THE DEATH DEALER

Matt Shayne, with his incredible gun skills, had done everything from bounty hunting to guarding trains, but those days had gone – or so he thought.

However, destiny had other plans for him, goaded by Red Backus he had no alternative but to shoot the arrogant young hardcase. Soon Matt had the remainder of the Backus clan baying for his blood. By bushwhacking or backstabbing it looked as if Matt's days were numbered.

THE DEATH DEALER

THE DEATH DEALER

by

Walt Drummond

Dales Large Print Books
Long Preston, North Yorkshire,
BD23 4ND, England.

British Library Cataloguing in Publication Data.

Drummond, Walt
    The death dealer.

    A catalogue record of this book is
    available from the British Library

    ISBN   1-84262-240-4 pbk

First published in Great Britain in 1974
Originally published in paperback as *The Death Dealer* by Wes
Yancey

Copyright © 1974, 2002 Norman Lazenby

Cover illustration © Faba by arrangement with
Norma Editorial S.A.

The right of Norman Lazenby to be identified as the author of
this work has been asserted by him in accordance with the
Copyright, Designs and Patents Act, 1988

Published in Large Print 2003 by arrangement with
Robert Hale Limited

Dales Large Print is an imprint of Library Magna Books Ltd.

Printed and bound in Great Britain by
T.J. (International) Ltd., Cornwall, PL28 8RW

1

A Boy And A Noose

He had been drinking hard for three days because of the killing, not that he gave a damn about the demise of Red Backus, but he felt bitter about the way he had broken the promises he had made to himself. He'd wanted to hang up the Colt sixgun, fix it good and proper on the pine-and-adobe wall of his ranchhouse and go about the business of raising beef. In fact, he had done just that for about two months, ever since he had taken over the small T-Bar-T ranch, but every weekend on his visit to town for a hand of cards and a convivial drink, he had had to put up with an unbelievably arrogant mixture of jeers and taunts from Red Backus.

The young hardcase's confidence in his speed with a handgun had been overrated. He had dropped during the double crack of guns, a slug in the chest, his own shot singing harmlessly into the sky.

The undertaker had carried the bleeding body away and the sheriff had stalked grimly back to his office. Matt Shayne had gone away for a drink – and he'd kept at it, bitterly for three days.

He'd worn his gun. His tie-hitched horse outside the saloon had been decorated with the long Winchester in the saddle scabbard.

He'd figured he would snap out of it in time. In fact, by about mid-week he was sick of the whiskey bottle, realizing he was a fool to neglect his newly acquired ranch. He could forget Red Backus, as he had forgotten the other dead men down the shadowy trails of his memory. What irked was the knowledge that he had not yet escaped from his gun-ridden past. He was still a gunslinger.

Then Sheriff Phil Peake had come to tell

him about the Backus family. 'They're in town – all three of 'em. Old man Bill Backus, his other son, Walt, and the girl.'

'Girl? What girl?' Matt raised dark eyebrows, his sunbrowned face showing hints of Apache blood.

'The girl is Liza Backus, sister to Red. Didn't you know?'

'Why the hell should I know about a family of no-account buzzards? Trappers, ain't they? That's all I was told...'

'Sure; they're wild.' The sheriff hitched his bolt, smoothed a thick walrus moustache and spoke raspingly, 'You'd be well advised to ride back to your spread, Matt Shayne, and avoid trouble. If you were a drifter, I'd tell you to leave town – but you've bought yourself into the community here at Three Forks.'

Matt Shayne got to his feet, jarring against the table. The bottle nearly fell over but he grabbed at it with a speed of reaction that the alcohol had not dulled. He grinned at the other man. 'You're pretty scared of me – that so, Sheriff Peake?'

'You've got a reputation…'

'Not in this town.'

'No – but you were known right through the territory. Matt Shayne, gun for hire. You worked for ranchers who had grudges or range wars on their hands. You guarded trains against the James brothers. You shot your way out of two card games, leaving two dead. And you did a bit of bounty huntin' – all gunmen's work. I didn't like it when you hit this town.'

Matt looked over the tall, heavily built lawman, seeing the distrust and caution in his black eyes. Phil Peake always wore an old work hat and a black jacket that had seen better days. The latter, a voluminous garment, half-hid his big, worn holster and heavy gun. He looked old, but he was about thirty, only two years older than Matt Shayne.

'Pick up your bottle and hightail it back to your spread,' advised the sheriff. 'Then, when Bill Backus and his son and daughter come for you with their buffalo guns, you'll at least be out of my sight and hearing.'

'I guess you're right.' Matt Shayne's grin challenged the sheriff. 'Say, I hope you find the Backus family, Phil, and do a little preaching to them. From what I hear, they could do with it more'n me.' He put on his hat. 'I'm a law-abiding citizen and I'm going home. *Adios,* and don't forget to send the Backus lot back to their hills.'

He went out with a slow, long-paced stride, his brown pants tight against wiry thighs, his black flannel shirt shrunk to a second skin. Men in the saloon watched him go and, returning to their drinks, shook their heads dubiously.

Phil Peake bought himself a drink. Matt Shayne halted on the boardwalk as the batwings swung behind him. A bright sun played on the yellow dust of Three Forks. A cool wind was coming down from the hills just ten miles north of this bend of the Pecos River.

He knew he should go home. He was clear out of remorse and the sheriff was right –

maybe a bit more riding would cool the Backus lot.

A woman hailed him from across the street. 'Why, hello, Matt. Are you trying to avoid me? I've been wondering if I should dive into that saloon and haul you out. You need some good female company, mister.'

She was standing in the shade: Violet Denton, owner of the hotel known as The Splendide, a place where the stage always halted and where travellers could find a comfortable room – and a lady friend for the night if so desired. It was Violet who made the arrangements.

He waved to her. She looked sweetly feminine in her long, trailing dress, her lush shape very much emphasised. As he walked over to her, he saw the pink in her cheeks and the brightness of her eyes. She was very assured and mature. She had been married, but the guy had got drunk one night and had broken his neck falling down the stairs. She had inherited the hotel, some money and another degree of maturity. She had told him about her life during the past eight weeks of their friendship and she had hinted that she didn't want to be a widow forever. He could see that, but there wasn't anything he intended to do about it. She was lovely, mature, and she knew men – and it showed. Maybe the last fact was responsible for the cautious way he had handled their friendship.

'I'm going back to my ranch,' he stated.

'Good for you. You're not really a drinking man.'

'I've been told to get out of town…'

The wind ruffled a wisp of her blonde hair. She tucked it back with an elegant hand. 'Come to my hotel and have coffee with me – or tea. Yes, I've really got tea…'

'That liquid ain't for me,' he clipped back with a laugh. 'Sorry, Violet – I'm goin'.'

'Red Backus had it coming,' she assured him.

'Maybe.' He looked past her, down the dusty street, beyond the wagons outside the freight office, down to the rickety premises that served the blacksmith at the far end of town. He'd seen three riders in black, straddling tired horses, and although he had never seen them before, a sixth sense warned him that their approach meant trouble for him.

As he stared she glanced in the same direction. Then, fear in her blue eyes, she said huskily, 'Get going, Matt. They'll kill you. That's Bill, Walt and Liza Backus. They're animals ... not as good as the creatures they trap ... and they live rough ... like goats in a barn.'

'I can't run.' His eyes shadowed by his hat, his lips tight, he watched the oddly slow gait of the approaching horses.

'They'll kill you – and that girl is as bad as her father and brother.'

'You *want me* to run?'

Violet Denton laid a hand on his shirtsleeve. 'Matt, you're no good to anyone dead. Please, Matt, just ride. Maybe they'll cool it off. Maybe the sheriff will warn them.'

He knew he stood a good chance of killing some of them if it came to a showdown. But three of them? And one a girl? Slowly shaking his head, he knew he didn't want any more killings.

He was on his horse when he threw another glance at the black shapes of the distant riders. Nearer, he saw the bearded face of the two men and the tanned oval of a girlish face. The impression gained, he heeled his horse forward and the long-legged animal went briskly down the main street of Three Forks.

Violet Denton pressed back against the clapboard of a building, her hand to her mouth. The three tired nags of the Backus family jerked into a full lope but this lasted only to the perimeter of the town and by then Matt Shayne was not in sight.

'We'll get him!' mouthed Bill Backus. 'Just see if we don't!'

Matt Shayne headed down the valley in a burst of drumming hoofs, the sun at his back, the alcohol fading from his mind. He knew the drinking and the remorse were over. He'd get control again, start working on the ton of chores he'd left at the T-Bar-T. What the hell had got into him, anyway? Red Backus would never have made old bones in any case.

He suddenly rode into the bunch of riders under the clump of twisted sycamore trees and saw the body jerking at the end of the length of hangman's rope.

At the same time he heard a boy's screams of terror and fury, as if sheer horror had suddenly loosened his tongue, and he saw the two men holding the lad with a force that was brutal.

One man sat his horse and watched the dangling body kick and writhe away the last moments of life. Another sat motionless in his saddle, a skinny little man with a lined, impassive face. Matt recognized him, vaguely. He was a townsman from Three Springs, but Matt could not recall his name.

Matt Shayne knew the big man on the horse. He was Caleb Dray, a rancher whose land was five times the size of the T-Bar-T. He was a big, bulky man, known to be hard and wealthy.

Matt Shayne snarled, 'Cut him down! I say, cut him down!'

'You can mind your own business!'

'Who gave you men the right to hold a lynching party?' It was a rhetorical question; more important was action. Matt jigged his horse close to the dying man and whipped out his knife from his belt. But the slash at the swaying rope missed by inches as the big man in the long frock-coat pushed his mount against the flank of Matt Shayne's animal.

'I know you, Shayne. You're the new-comer. Get outa here and mind your own blamed business. This is Mick Skinner we're hangin'...'

'You got no legal right to hang anybody!' Face set, angled in taut lines, Matt made another attempt to save the life of the wretched man. But Caleb Dray blocked him again. What was more significant, a Colt appeared in his hand.

Face twisted in distaste, Matt looked momentarily at the hanging man and saw the signs of death in the protruding eyes, the tongue that seemed to be trying to escape the contorted mouth. The body had quit twitching. Maybe there was a flicker of life in it, maybe not.

The boy screamed again. 'Stop 'em! Stop 'em, mister! That's my pa – my pa! He ain't done nothin' wrong!'

'He's a rustling, murderous rogue,' said the thin man in an unpleasant, reedy voice.

'And a horse thief,' snapped Caleb Dray. 'But he's changed his last brand.'

'Ask anybody in these parts,' the skinny little man said. 'For fifty miles around … year after year … thievin' and lying … never done a day's work in his life…'

'Get him down!' Matt Shayne shouted. 'Get to hell outa my way! You–'

'He's dead,' Caleb Dray announced. He fastened bleak eyes on Matt. 'Get on your way. You can't help him.'

'My pa!' shrilled the boy. 'He ain't dead … mister … he ain't … is he, mister?'

Suddenly, feeling his mouth was full of dirt, Matt Shayne jigged his horse forward and made a final thrust with his knife, disregarding the big man's gun. The blade nicked easily through the manila, just above the hangman's knot. The body fell to the ground and lay without a twitch. Matt was beside the hanged man in seconds.

'My pa!' The boy twisted in the grip of the two men like a wild animal. Matt felt for heartbeats and then for a pulse. There was no sign of life. He looked up heavily at the two mounted men.

'I think he's dead.'

Screams of rage tore from the boy's throat. 'I'll kill you dirty bullies – just see if I don't! I'll get me a gun. I'll kill you!'

One of the men holding the boy turned to Caleb Dray. 'If you ask me, the boy should go the same way…'

Caleb Dray seemed to stiffen and become a hard mould on a saddle. 'He's just a boy…'

'He's got the same wild blood. He's right – he'll kill us. He'll grow up – he won't forget – his thievin', murderin' kind never do.'

'We can't hang a boy.' The words grated reluctantly from the big man's lips.

'He'll remember us,' muttered the man who was holding the lad. 'Hell, we won't be able to sleep. He could sneak up on us at night … in the bunkhouse, Mr Dray … think of that…'

'You work for me and I'll see that you're all right. Two grown men can't be scared of a boy. Granted he's got his father's sneaky blood and bad ways and if he grows up to be another Mick Skinner maybe he'll end up dangling like his damned parent. Fact is, maybe we'll get around to do just that in a few years' time.'

Matt Shayne got to his feet. His hand hovered like a claw over his walnut-butted gun. 'You'll take your hands off that boy – and I'll give you no more'n five seconds to do it.'

The lad was released. The two rangehands

glared at Matt Shayne, work-lined visages showing the realization that here was a gunman. The boy darted over to the body of his father and huddled over him, his rage giving way to sobs.

Caleb Dray fixed his speculative gaze on Matt Shayne. 'Why don't you just ride on, man?'

'I want to make sure the boy's not harmed.'

'I'll give you my word that he won't be touched,' said the other flatly. 'He won't follow his father, at least not for a few years.'

'You set yourself up as judge and hangman, huh?' Matt retorted. 'You must know that I'll report this lynchin' to the sheriff in Three Forks – and you know that lynching ain't legal.'

Caleb Dray nodded. 'That's right for most parts of the territory, but around this valley there's a tradition that lynchin' can be justified. And in this case, Shayne, everybody knows Mick Skinner for a miserable thief.'

'Then he should have been tried – given a hearin'.'

'He convicted himself for years. But you go to the sheriff if you want. It won't mean a thing…'

Like an enraged mountain cat, the boy sprang to life. He shot across the ground, his denim-clad legs pistoning. He hurled himself at Caleb Dray, grabbing at the man's stirruped boot. He tried to tug the man from his horse, crying: 'You put the rope around my pa! You did it! I'm goin' to kill you some day – just see if I don't!'

Matt went over to the boy and held his shoulders. 'Come on, kid. I know you've had a terrible shock, but there ain't nothing you can do now.'

The boy turned on him, his smooth face contorted into a mask. 'Nobody will stop me! I'll kill these men – all of 'em!'

'Come on, boy. Ride along with me,' said Matt gently. 'You can stick with me for a day ar two.'

'Watch him,' said the thin little man. 'He comes of bad stock. Bad seed … worse than a rat … he should be dead … like his pa.'

24

2

Attempted Showdown

'You can help me dig a grave – right here,' said Matt. He watched the boy. 'What's your full name?'

'Jimmy Skinner.' The lad raised his gaze from his father's body, a bleak look on his thin face. He stared down once more, almost disbelievingly.

'How old are you?' Matt Shayne began to dig at the earth with his long-bladed knife.

'I'm twelve.' Then, looking up again, eyes flaring into brightness. 'I *will* kill those dirty rats! I *will!*'

Matt pointed to a thick stick under the sycamore. 'Use that and dig. Where do you live, boy?'

'We got a cabin in Bitter Canyon.'

'Do you get any schooling in town?'

'It ain't no good. My pa said it ain't for the likes of me.'

'Get that stick,' said Matt sternly. 'We got work to do. And stop snufflin'. We bury him here – and, well, I'll say a few words over the grave. I'm not goin' back to town just yet, so you can come with me to my ranch.'

'Not me, mister. I'm goin' back to the cabin.'

'You can't live alone.' Matt stabbed at the soft earth and scooped soil to one side. 'Anyway, those hired hands of Caleb Dray might just decide to pay you a visit. They're afraid of you, boy, and fear pushes some galoots to extreme measures. Yeah, they're afraid you'll sneak up on 'em some night. They want you dead.'

The boy stabbed at the earth and gulped. 'I'll kill 'em first. I know how to. Pa showed me how to use guns...'

Some time later the body was laid in the shallow grave and stones placed over the spot. Matt Shayne said a few curt words he remembered from a burial service and watched the boy. He figured he was all set to cry, so he tapped his shoulder and turned. 'Come on, get to my horse. We're goin'.'

'I ain't goin' to your ranch!' Jimmy cried. 'I'm a Skinner, a no-account – bad blood – you heard what they said! I steal and I lie my head off! And I ain't ridin' with you, mister!'

'That's what you think,' said Matt Shayne, and he wrapped an arm around the boy that was like an iron band. The youngster's ensuing struggles were to no avail. Jimmy Skinner was placed on the saddle of the long-legged, nervy horse and Matt got up behind him. The mount leaped away from the sycamore grove.

That night, in the small ranchhouse of the T-Bar-T, which Matt ran with the help of two elderly punchers, he heard the boy crying in the spare bedroom. He let him cry it out; it was better that way. Soft-soaping the boy would be no good.

In the morning he decided to see the sheriff and make some pointed remarks about the legality of lynching. And Jimmy would come along with him. He couldn't leave the boy on his own at the ranch. He might hit the trail and get into trouble. He might even steal a gun. Anyway, Phil Peake could question the boy.

They rode in just before midday, the sun rising hot, the wind from the hills no longer cool. Three Forks was bustling with activity. Freight wagons were being loaded and unloaded, and the stage to Lamesa was ready to pull out with a passenger list of six – two cattle buyers, a drummer with his carpetbag, two ladies in silk dresses who were known in the better class saloons of Three Forks and Lamesa as willing to please, and a gambler who had been told to leave town.

As they got to the main stem they heard banjos, badly played trumpets and a drum that crashed like a charge of dynamite. They saw a small crowd of gaping onlookers around the band, above which a banner proclaimed: 'Waldo's Circus. Now In Town.'

28

'Now that's somethin',' said Matt. 'You like a circus, boy?'

'Ain't never heard of 'em. What is it?'

'Oh, clowns and animals and lots of fun. Say, maybe you can go after we've seen the sheriff. Seems they've got a tent on the outskirts of town.'

'I don't want to.' The boy sat his horse grimly. 'I know what I aim to do.'

'You're sticking with me, Jimmy – and no tricks.'

When the animals were hitched at the tie rail, they went into the sheriff's office, boots scuffing the bare wood floor. Phil Peake looked around from the rifle case he was locking. He nodded.

'I heard. Dray told me.'

Matt shut the door, placed one booted foot on a chair and leaned forward. 'He lynched this boy's father. He figured he had the right.'

'He probably did.'

'Lynching is murder in most territories. Are you tryin' to tell me the law is different around here?'

'You're a newcomer, Shayne,' said Sheriff Phil Peake heavily. 'So I'll explain. There's a tradition around here goin' back to the old days. Settlements had no lawmen of any sort, so leading citizens took matters into their own hands. I admit it's been a long time since the last necktie party, but–'

'It's all right by you – this killing of Mick Skinner?'

The sheriff spread his hands. 'Look, he had it coming. He's been in this jail half a dozen times. He stole horses, faked the brands and got away with it, time and time again. In town he'd steal money from drunks.'

'So you ain't goin' to do a thing about it?'

'What do you want me to do, arrest Caleb Dray? He's the biggest rancher around here. Skinner lived off him for years.'

'Big man, huh? That's all that matters. Do you know that Dray's hands wanted to string up this boy?'

Phil Peake scowled. 'Dray didn't mention that.'

'Well, he ordered them to cool off,' Matt admitted. 'But I'll tell you something, Mr Lawman. If this boy is harmed in any way, I'll hold Dray responsible – and you, too, Sheriff. Right. You've been told.'

'And I'm tellin' you something, Shayne,' said the sheriff angrily. 'That Backus family is still in town and I hear they want you dead. I'll not have any feudin' inside the town boundaries – so you'd better ride out.'

'Have you said the same to the Backus bunch?'

'I have. So watch it, Shayne. And that boy – you know there's talk of puttin' him into a home?'

'Whose talk?'

'Just folks who knew the father. Honest people were sick and tired of Mick Skinner. They say the boy is just as bad, and that sooner or later blood will tell. He's the son of a thief.'

'He ain't going into no home,' said Matt firmly.

'How come? You aim to take care of him?'

31

'Maybe ... for the time being, anyhow.'

'You'll end up having a lot of people disliking you. I mean just ordinary folks, plus Caleb Dray and his hands. And you've also got the Backus family wantin' your blood, Shayne. You sure have made a queer start around here.'

Matt dropped his boot onto the worn floor. 'Maybe I'll finish all right. But I'll be on my best behaviour and maybe everybody will cool off. All I want to do, anyway, is raise cattle...'

Sheriff Phil Peake watched Shayne go with the boy and muttered, 'Yeah, but you're a gunman, Shayne, and you'll go for a hogleg when the trouble comes. You've still got the instinct...'

Matt led the boy along the main street. The band from the circus was still making plenty of noise. Matt grinned and looked down at Jimmy Skinner.

'Now this circus... I saw a big one in San Antonio and was mighty taken up by a lady horse-rider...' He coughed. 'Wal, never mind that – I reckon we could have something to eat and then mosey along to this circus, huh?'

'If you want,' said the boy indifferently.

Matt looked at the boy's thin frame. 'I think you need steak, boy. And maybe a glass of milk.'

'I always drank coffee with my pa.'

'Sure, but you need fillin' out. I've seen more meat on a beanstalk. Now–' They were walking slowly down the street and there was a saloon just ten yards ahead. Matt knew the place. The Big Chance, a typical batwinged establishment where drink flowed and gaming continued until the early hours of any day. There were three saloons in Three Forks. The town was growing. The Splendide was built mainly of brick, just like the banks. The Big Chance, however, catered for men of rough tastes in both accommodation and booze.

Matt Shayne saw them emerge from the batwings; three dark-clad shapes, the girl noticeable as such because of her smooth face and slighter build. The shirt of the older man – Bill Backus – was once grey, but sweat, dust and food grease had darkened it. A black hat and a black-bearded face helped the illusion of grimness. Walt Backus was nothing more than a younger version of his father, except that he owned a good set of white teeth. Right now they were exposed in a humourless leer.

Matt's attention shifted to Liza Backus and stayed fixed on her for what seemed a long time. Maybe the girl's clothes were as disreputable as those of her father and brother, but there was an animalish quality, highly female, about her stance and attitude towards the man before her. She was the first to speak.

'You – the dirty killer! Well, we got you to rights. You'll pay for killin' Red!'

Matt held his smile. He saw the hands-on-hip posture, the shapeless old Stetson hanging at the back of her neck, held by a thong around her smooth throat. He saw the polished stock of the sixgun snug in a holster, and the leather gunbelt that would have looked fine on a young man. He saw the smudges of trail dirt on her face and figured she thought of washing as an extravagance. She was a woman trying to emulate a roughneck father who lived by slaughtering creatures of the wild and she'd had two brothers who knew no better.

'You gunned down my lad!' Bill Backus flung the accusation like an obscenity.

'We been watchin' for you,' added Walt. 'We figured to ride out to your spread, but now you saved us the trouble. We aim to kill you.'

'Red was killed in a fair fight,' said Matt evenly.

'You goddamn liar!' Walt cried.

Matt tried again. 'One of you will die – maybe two – if you go for those hoglegs.'

Bill Backus twisted his head to look first at his son, and then at his daughter. 'Spread out. We'll get him. Fan out – he can't watch three of us.'

They began to edge away from each other.

The girl stepped to the right, into the street. Walt Backus inched down the boardwalk. The father scuffled his dirty worn boots backwards. For the moment, hands stayed clear of gun butts.

Matt tapped the boy's shoulder. 'You get out of this. Just walk away. Don't run. They've got no quarrel with you.'

'They'll – they'll kill you,' breathed the boy.

'Maybe.' Matt didn't take his eyes off the three. 'Now scat.'

As the boys moved slowly away, Bill Backus said, 'That's Mick Skinner's brat. I knowed him. Now what's he doin' with a rat like you? Well, it don't matter.'

People on the street had halted to stare at Matt Shayne and the vengeful Backus trio. Then the people began to crowd into doorways and edge around corners. A gig coming down the main stem drew up and the driver hurriedly tried to turn the carriage.

Matt felt slow anger boil into his throat.

He threw warnings to the trapper family. 'I'll get two of you, so help me! You want to die?'

'We aim to get you first,' snarled Bill Backus. 'You don't look so hell-fired quick to me. I seen gunnies. A real killer would have gone for his hardware and chopped us down afore now.'

Matt Shayne felt the weight of his Colt against his thigh. The man was right. He should draw now before they fanned out too far. He was letting them steal the main trick. Soon one of them would be almost behind him.

He turned, trying to face all three, but the girl was right across the road. How good was she with a gun? Did she have the killer stamp in her?

Walt Backus was inching along the boardwalk. Pretty soon he'd be behind the man he hated. The father of the blood-hungry two was at centre point, motionless now. Maybe he wasn't a professional gunman, but he knew how to circle his prey.

For some reason Matt glanced with narrowed eyes at the girl again. He knew he wouldn't trigger at her; he'd be too busy diving, snapping shots at the two men. His only chance was to keep moving the moment his hand clawed for the gun. Maybe it would be the girl who'd get him. Matt Shayne, killed by a girl. It was a hell of a thought.

He didn't hate this Backus family. He just wished to God they'd disappear. They were forcing him back to the gun, making him break his promise to himself.

He was ready to jerk into action when the sheriff came striding angrily onto the scene, his rifle cradled low. His walrus moustache jerked as he bawled, 'Hold it! By Gawd, I'll blast the first one that moves a finger!'

Nothing moved. Walking closer, Phil Peake got to a position where he threatened all four would-be combatants before he went on: 'Drop those gunbelts! I mean it! I'll shoot to kill at the first trick.'

The two Backus men frowned heavily. The

girl's eyes, dark as a gypsy's, sparked anger at the sheriff.

'This is a private fight, lawman. Keep out.'

'You're a fool, young lady,' said Phil Peake. 'You're takin' on a real gunhand – one Matt Shayne. He's out-gunned more men than you've had hot baths. You'd end up an orphan, lady. Now I ain't foolin' – drop those damned gunbelts.'

Matt Shayne was the first to comply. His belt hit the dust and he smiled thinly as he watched the Backus men struggle with fear and fury. Then the girl slowly unbuckled her belt and dropped it, gun in holster. It rested near the boardwalk.

Bill Backus and his son slowly got rid of their belts. Phil Peake rapped an order to a man in a doorway:

'Medway, get that damned artillery. Pick it up.' He waited, a smile creeping across his face. 'Now you people can have a real fight if you like – somethin' that will entertain folks and maybe get rid of the bad blood between you.' He paused, watching Medway pick up the last of the gunware. Then he went on in a sour note: 'I ain't objecting to a skirmish right here and now in the dust. I guess it's two to one, but I didn't pick the odds. OK, belt hell out of each other – and then get out of my town.'

If Phil Peake thought the fight was only two to one, he was taken by surprise. The girl was first to rush in.

Shayne would have hesitated before putting a bullet into her soft skin, but he stopped her furious onslaught immediately with a rough shove that sent her sprawling in the dusty road. A roar of enjoyment went up from male throats around the scene while one or two women emitted tiny screams. As Liza Backus slid her shapely rump along the dust, the two men barged in, ready to maim even if they couldn't kill. Matt whirled to face them. He knew something about roughhouses, having been thrown into a few at an early age, and he also knew a lot about boxing. He'd learned under an ex-army sergeant who had boxed with the best. The man had taught him the value of a straight left and a right hook.

It was the left that got through to Walt Backus' face and sent him staggering back as if a pole had rammed him. Then Matt turned to the old man who had been trying to throw an arm around his neck. Matt hit Bill Backus low enough to hurt but high enough to avoid the label of foul. Bill Backus gasped, almost spewed, and his arms sagged. Matt hit him twice between the glaring eyes for a starter and then in the mouth. Old yellowed teeth loosened and almost choked the old-timer. He went sprawling back, unable to keep his balance, and he hit the rutted road on his back.

Then it was Liza Backus again. She rushed at him, a little scream of rage escaping her. Liza's fingers were curled like claws. But Matt Shayne went under those clawing hands, then he straightened and she ran right into his arms.

He held her while she clawed and kicked at him. He avoided the raking fingernails, grabbed one arm and bent it back as a man in the crowd yelled, 'Give the she-cat a good hiding on the backside, mister!' Laughter went up.

But grappling with a wild girl was no joke to Matt Shayne. He twisted her arms behind her and pushed her towards a horse trough. The crowd cheered as she fell into the trough. He held her head down until he sensed the raging assault of Walt Backus. The man ran into Matt like a charging steer, wrapping his strong arms around him. He tried to throw Matt. His idea was to get his opponent on the ground, the usual place for the loser in a roughhouse.

Matt didn't comply with the rules in dealing with this man. He brought his knee up and heard Walt Backus grunt in pain. Then he kicked at the shins. Walt Backus howled this time and jigged back. Matt bunched two fists together and used them like a battering ram on the man's head. Walt Backus fell back to the road, unconscious.

Liza Backus had struggled out of the water

trough and was glaring her hatred at Shayne. Bill Backus had hauled himself up by means of a veranda upright and was swallowing blood and bile.

Phil Peake took a look at the scene and thought it was time he asserted his authority. 'All right, you're all goin' to jail for fightin' in the street. That'll cool you off, I guess.'

3

The Sweatshop

Matt Shayne sat quietly in his cell for some time, wiping his mouth and examining a barked knuckle. Across the stone-slabbed passage the three members of the Backus family sat behind bars and glared their hatred at him. They had run out of verbal threats.

After an hour of the cooling-off process, Matt found himself stealing curious glances at Liza Backus. The girl sat on a wooden bench, tense, not moving. Her hat was at the back of her head and her dark hair fell raggedly, unattractively. The jeans she wore were too baggy for a girl. Only the worn shirt gave any real hint of her sex. There were two rounded bulges that slowly rose and fell as she breathed. But it wasn't just that which dragged curiosity from Matt Shayne; it was the thought that there might be something likeable deep down in the rough, animal-like role the girl had assumed. He couldn't explain it. Maybe it was simply because she was a woman.

After some time he figured Phil Peake had squeezed the last bit out of his assertion of authority, so he began to yell for the sheriff. A deputy came.

'I want out,' Shayne said.

'Phil ain't back yet. I'm not turning those keys.'

'The hell with you,' Matt snapped. 'I've got work to do. And where's the boy, Jimmy Skinner?'

'Maybe doin' a bit of thievin',' said the deputy sourly. 'He was brought up to it, I know that for sure. Little devil.'

'You'd be a thief, too, if you'd been taught nothin' else,' said Matt. 'Get Peake. I want out of here.'

The snarled orders didn't endear him to

the deputy, but he couldn't care less about that. He was tired of the cell and he figured the charade had been played out long enough.

Besides, there was a rank smell coming from the two Backus men.

The sun was low when he finally got out of the cell, to the accompaniment of threats from Bill and Walt Backus. In the office, Phil Peake handed him his gun and belt. And some advice: 'You better head for your spread. I had to treat you the same as that bunch of hillside varmints. I sure hope you'll avoid them in the future. I want law and order in Three Forks – and you did kill a man.'

'I've killed thirteen,' said Matt Shayne flatly. 'The boy – where did he go?'

He saw a cold light flash in Sheriff Phil Peake's eyes. 'Ride out, Shayne. Mind your own business.'

'Where is Jimmy Skinner?'

'He was rounded up, taken to Roper Stell's place.'

'Who the hell is Roper Stell?'

'He owns a little workshop on the edge of the town. He employs two men and three other lads, making anythin' in metal, like iron ploughs for them nesters over in the east and railings for big ranchers to decorate verandas. Guns, too, and some locksmith work. Almost anythin' in iron.'

Suddenly Matt's mind went back to the hanging, to the skinny little man whose name he could not recall. Now he knew. Roper Stell. Angrily he asked, 'Why did you give Jimmy to him?'

Phil Peake stared back. 'Ain't an honest trade better than stealin'? Roper Stell will keep him working. The boy won't have time to plague other folks.'

'Is that so?' Matt Shayne shook his head. 'I don't think this Roper Stell is good for that boy. He said Jimmy ought to be hanged. I heard him say it. Now why does he want to take the boy into his care?'

'Stell is a man of influence – a manufacturer. He's on the town committee.

He'll make that boy toe the line, you'll see.'

'I will see, Sheriff. I'll see into it right now.' Matt tightened his gunbelt. 'This Roper Stell was a leading guest at the necktie party. I don't think it was wise to hand the boy into his care.'

'I ain't asking your opinion,' snapped Phil Peake. 'It's done. Stell offered to take the lad and that was it.'

Matt jerked a nod in the direction of the cells. 'What about the Backus bunch? Don't they warrant their freedom?'

'Why should you worry? They're stayin' the night. Sure, I'm leaning on 'em, but they're not the most desirable citizens in this territory. They'll get out in the morning. They'll also get fed. Hell, ain't that somethin'?'

Shaking his head, Matt went to collect his horse. The animal had kicked a hole in the dirt road, not being the most patient of beasts. A snicker and a show of teeth welcomed Matt. The horse nuzzled his arm as he came close. He knew the animal needed feeding and that would come pretty soon, after he had visited Roper Stell's place.

After an enquiry, he found the dirty, ramshackle workshop standing near a shack owned by a one-man printing business. A rundown livery huddled close to the two buildings. A rubbish tip occupied a hollow in the land some yards away. Near the hollow a town Indian squatted outside his shack and watched his hens strut around the area. Hearing a noise from the workshop, Matt walked purposefully forward, figuring to assess the situation for himself.

Something nagged at him. Why should Stell want to do anything good for the Skinner boy after the things he'd said about his bad blood and parentage? From what he had seen of the skinny little man, there didn't seem much generosity in his makeup.

Matt Shayne walked through a battered, grimy door that swung on twisted hinges. He stared around the gloomy interior of the workshop, his nostrils assailed by fumes and the grit-filled air. Primitive, hand-operated machines were clanking and punching. Two boys with sooty faces were trying to lift a heavy length of rail onto a chipped work-bench and it was obviously beyond their combined strength. Matt stepped forward and hefted the ornamental rail section into place. The boys stared at him, their faces paling under the grime. They bent again to handle another length of railing. Matt helped them, noting the weight.

'Ain't you got hoists here?' he rapped. 'You kids want to break your backs?'

'Mr Stell says we can manage,' mumbled a boy.

Matt moved on. He was aware that metalwork and dirt went hand in hand, but this cavernous shed wasn't fit for animals. He spotted Jimmy Skinner at the far end, using a three-pound hammer on some object. Matt walked over. 'Hey, boy! Do you like this place?'

'I hate it, Mr Shayne!' The answer burst from the lad. 'Look at it! I've been here three hours … coughing all the time, what with all the dust. Get me outa here. Roper Stell says I'll have to work for my keep … sleep in a room with the other lads at the back of here…'

Matt flung a grim glance at the other two. 'They don't look more'n twelve years old. So this is the manufacturer's hellhole. I know a slave shop when I see it, Jimmy. You're gettin' out. This ain't no place for a boy – and it sure ain't no substitute for fresh air and grassland.'

An elderly man in a leather apron quit working at a forge and hurried away. He had gone to fetch his boss, Matt surmised, and minutes later he saw he was right. Roper Stell walked into the dirty cavern, his beaky face angry, his hands holding the lapels of his coat. The leather-aproned individual was behind him – and so was another man, a huge character in a plaid shirt and leather pants.

'You are trespassing, sir,' squealed Roper Stell. 'Get out.'

'I'm taking Jimmy Skinner with me.'

'You are not, sir. He is about to be indentured with me. I shall take charge of him, see that he earns his bread and butter.'

Matt laughed sourly. 'You lousy little hypocrite – you're running a sweat shop and you want labour that costs you nothing.'

'He'll learn a trade and that's a valuable thing,' piped Roper Stell. 'A man like you – a gunhand – has no right to talk. I offer boys a chance to learn something.'

'You offer them slavery. Why the hell don't you get some fresh air into this hole? And how can anyone see in this half-light? You want 'em to end up blind?'

'Get out of here, my man.'

'Sure. But I'm taking Jimmy. Seems you changed your mind about wantin' him dead, huh? Figured to break him another way?'

Roper Stell's sparse frame shook like a vindictive skeleton. He whipped around. 'Put him out, Novak.'

The big man in the plaid shirt and leather pants advanced, his hands outstretched like a wrestler's. A smile decorated his wide, round face. He was curiously hairless, Matt Shayne noted. Then the fellow gave out cries of childish delight. He was evidently pleased to be able to use his strength. Novak made a surprisingly swift leap and in a flash his hands were on Matt's shoulders. A heave and Matt thudded to the dusty floor.

Novak stood over him, grinning, ready, confident.

Matt Shayne looked up, knowing he could draw his gun and kill the man. But the fellow was unarmed. Matt suddenly kicked out and his boots slammed hard into the other's legs.

The kick should have hurt, but the leather pants absorbed much of it. The man jumped back. Matt got to his feet, knowing there was no escape unless he used his gun.

The next rush came. Matt dodged at the last second, wheeling and ramming two blows – a right and a left – at the back of the man's hairless neck. They were blows that should have hurt any normal man, but

Novak just bunched his shoulder muscles and turned. He crouched and inched forward. Matt lashed out when the hulking body came within punching range. A left, a right, another left, then a savage looking right. But Novak just shook his head, then he wrapped his arms around Matt.

'Break him, Novak!' squeaked Roper Stell. 'Smash him and then throw him out. He has no right to be here. He's a trespasser, and we can deal with him as we like.'

Matt couldn't move. He wished he had drawn his gun. It lay in the holster, inches from his hand, but he couldn't move his arm. Novak increased the pressure, and his round face grinned. Matt tried to rock free of the big, bald man. But he didn't have the other's weight and couldn't get him off-balance. Then he tried to crook a leg around Novak's ankle, tried to kick away his balance. But the legs stood like stone pillars in the grime of the workshop.

Then young Jimmy Skinner took a hand. He picked up a length of metal bar and sprang at Novak, using the billet like a club on the man's skull. Novak sagged slowly, his weight now heaving on Matt Shayne. Roper Stell screamed hysterically and shook a bony fist at Jimmy. But he looked frightened as Novak slowly sank and Matt hunched back, free.

'I'll have the law on you!' the little man whined. 'Trespassing, assaulting my man, threatening me—'

'Let's make a job of it,' said Matt, and he grabbed the small man. 'Eat your own dust, *hombre*. Taste it.' And he pushed Stell down until his face was deep in the grime. Stell sucked in mouthfuls of the muck as he gasped and struggled. Novak lay quite still. The boys at the end of the shed huddled in fear and the forgeman backed to the shadows.

'Out,' Matt said. 'I think we ought to make ourselves scarce, Jimmy boy. We ain't gonna be too popular in Three Forks.'

'Have I killed that big feller?' the boy asked.

'No. He's out cold.'

'I'd like to kill him.'

Matt grabbed Jimmy's shirt collar. 'You can start forgettin' that word. It comes too damn quick to your lips.'

'My pa would've killed him…'

'Your pa got strung up…' Matt winced and wished he'd minded his tongue when he saw the boy's face twist in a bitter expression. 'Aw, come on. Let's get.'

The pair went out to the horse. The boy mounted behind Matt, hanging onto his gunbelt. As Matt jigged the horse forward, he took a backward glance. Roper Stell was outside the work shed, shaking his fist and promising retribution in a shrill voice.

Jimmy had entered town on a horse of his own. Matt went to the livery behind the sheriff's office on a hunch that the nag would be there. It was. He saddled it and waved curtly to the oldster minding the place. A few moments later he and Jimmy were riding out of town. It would be dark before they reached the T-Bar-T.

Roper Stell lost little time in seeking out Phil Peake and handing him his version of what had happened. The sheriff was in the bar of the Royal Hotel, a small room where men of some means congregated for drinks and conversation that wouldn't be interrupted by drunken punchers.

'That damned gunny – he's taken the boy away – near choked me to death. And that young squirt is a danger to decent folks. He tried to kill Novak – hit him with a metal bar–'

'Did you sign the indentures?' The sheriff looked at the rage-filled little man and thought, not for the first time, that he looked like a leathery vulture.

'I didn't have time, Mr Peake. I set the boy to work – figured to have him set his mark to paper tomorrow.'

'Then he ain't bound to you yet.' Phil Peake toyed with his glass of whiskey. 'I'll look into it.'

'First light,' said Roper Stell threateningly.

'You do it first thing tomorrow.'

Phil Peake turned sourly. 'You think I sit on my rump waitin' for your orders, Stell? I have plenty of duties all yellin' for my attention.'

'I'm a committeeman! I want service from you! I have influence.'

'I know. You and Caleb Dray appoint the sheriff in this town. All right, I'll tell Shayne to bring the kid back to town.'

'He should be jailed for assault.'

'Yeah, sure. Well, Mr Stell, I'm entitled to some time off and it's been a long day. I'm waiting for a good friend to drop in here.'

The dismissal was plain. Stell went out, his frail body quivering with rage.

At home that night, Matt Shayne forced the boy to have a bath in the large wooden tub which was shaped like a small ark. With steam rising, carbolic soap and scrubber handy, he kept the youth soaking. 'You'll get used to the idea, youngster. A bath a week is mighty fine for a feller your age...'

'Is that what you do?' Jimmy demanded to know.

Matt scowled. 'I bath when I hanker for it. Now shut up, get out and dry up. We're gonna do some reading.'

'My pa was no readin' man.'

'Your pa ain't no more,' said Matt harshly. 'You'd best think about that. You're goin' to school, too.'

The boy stopped drying his wiry body and pointed to the glass-fronted rifle case on the ranchhouse wall. A Greener shotgun, a Winchester and an old trade musket of .69 calibre which was more than a curio than a shooting iron, lay in the case. 'I'd sooner learn how to fire them guns, Mr Shayne. And that Colt you wear – that's a real neat gun.'

Matt shook his head. 'Boy, the day of the gun will be over by the time you're twenty-one. The signs are all around. You'd do better to learn to read.'

'But what's the use of that?'

It was an hour later, after an exasperating attempt to teach Jimmy how to read some simple words, that Matt sat for some time and smoked his long pipe. It was a luxury he owned to only when in an armchair. The smoke ended, he walked thoughtfully around the large room and stopped at the chair over which he had slung his gunbelt. The Colt was missing.

He frowned and went to the other bedroom. In the light from the living-room oil-lamp he saw the missing gun half hidden under the boy's pillow. He withdrew the weapon gently, leaving Jimmy sound asleep.

4

A Backus Dies

The Backus family hit the main street early in the day after a meagre breakfast that certainly didn't please them. Sheriff Phil Peake showed them to the door, his hand on his gunbutt as he said, 'Take my advice – head back to the hills and earn an honest dollar. Remember, if it wasn't for me then at least two of you would be dead right now and Matt Shayne would be in bad with me and the townspeople.' Phil Peake prodded a finger against Bill Backus' chest. 'This is a law-abiding town, feller. If you want to kill somebody, you do it elsewhere.'

Bill Backus collected his horses and took his son and daughter out of town. Thoughts of Matt Shayne rankled in his mind. He had a swollen nose and a cracked lip that added to the sourness in his gut. 'Let's finish with that gent. I aim to shoot him to rags.'

As they rode their broken-spirited horses, Walt added his bitter comment: 'We'll salivate him, sure thing – and we'll burn that damned ranch of his to the ground. We'll get him this time.'

Liza Backus rode her animal in silence, her lips compressed. She knew she hated deeply and there weren't words for it. It wasn't just her brother's death any longer; she just hated the mental image of the tall, lean man who had humiliated her by ducking her in the trough. The gun on her thigh seemed eager for her hand. She knew she'd kill and scream out in delight. She'd empty the gun into him. She'd watch him writhe and she'd laugh and laugh.

The trail led them over rolling country, grassy valleys and through stands of timber. There were cattle to be seen in nearly every hollow. Parts of this range were shared by ranchers; the T-Bar-T spread was in a narrow valley that started about ten miles out of town and became part of the rocky foot hills leading to the mountains.

'We'll kill him,' said Bill Backus for the tenth time. 'Just fill him with lead and watch the swine die. I'd like to carve 'im with a Bowie – but I figure we won't have time. We gotta get back to the hills and trap us some pelts.'

'Yeah, but we ain't goin' to take chances,' said Walt. 'He's a gunny. Used to hire out, I hear. We'll gut-fill him like he was a mangy wolf.'

The Backus three were not the only people who hated Matt Shayne at that moment. The diminutive Roper Stell was seething with anger at the way he had been treated. His face had been literally rubbed in the dirt. He, a leading man in the community! His frame was spare and his heart mean, but he had a pride that was big enough for the most bombastic man in town. So he went to see the sheriff again, almost before that worthy had had time to digest his breakfast.

'You getting out to that hellion's ranch?'

Phil Peake heaved his big body out of the comfortable leather chair that stood behind his office desk. 'You mean Shayne?'

'Who else?' barked Roper Stell.

The lawman breathed deeply. 'You know, Stell, because you didn't indenture that boy you ain't really got a claim on him.'

'I'm ready to put him to work – make a man out of him – teach him to work hard for his keep.'

'That you will, from all I hear. But I can't ride out there on a thin claim. I think we oughta see Judge Bunch – get his opinion.'

'He's out of town – on the circuit.'

'All right, we'll see him when he gets back.'

'That'll be in two days.'

'Waal, that young devil will keep, won't he? I ain't riding out until I've seen the judge and gotten some legal advice. I don't usually hell around with orphans.'

Almost exploding with this affront to his

pride, the little man strode away, black pants flapping. As he went, he mouthed aloud: 'If you won't take action, Mr Sheriff, then I will. I'll get that lad back – and God help him when I do!' His thoughts were now an obsession. And he knew who he could hire. Yeah, he'd get Bunt Garriga, who could handle a gun with the best of them.

On the T-Bar-T, Matt Shayne was watching young Jimmy eat a man-sized breakfast. He marvelled at how well the lad looked. After the bath, his skin seemed two shades lighter. Well, he'd have to find him some chores to do around the spread, something that would be healthy and interesting. And there was work for himself; he wanted to ride out to the fenced-off rock heaps at the northern end of the valley. He'd had trouble with young calves trapping themselves in those rocky clefts and he wanted to make sure that the fence was all right. Maybe it needed lengthening. And he had to set out work for Sam Harper and Manuel Reyna, the two hands he employed.

Matt showed Jimmy the tackroom, a small shack near the horse corral. He said, 'You could rub grease into some of these leathers. They look dry and ready to crack. And sort out the saddles – just tidy the place up a bit, Jimmy.'

'I'd sooner ride with you,' the youngster said.

Matt laughed. 'You know, we've all got to knuckle down to orders some time or other. Me – I give myself orders and it ain't always easy to obey them. Now you just get acquainted with this tackroom. You'll find it interesting once you start. I'll be gone for some time.'

'I always went out with pa...'

'Sure.' Matt paused. 'Was he good to you?'

'Well, sometimes he lathered me ... when he got drunk. But I didn't mind...'

Matt patted the boy's shoulder. Then he went out, mounted up, and told his waiting hands what to do before he headed his horse into a canter. He had a coil of wire around the saddle horn, wrapped with old canvas to prevent the barbs doing damage, and he had some tools in an old carpetbag which was slung around the rear of his saddle. He'd get some chores done; enough time had been lost one way and another.

It was about four hours later when he got back, hungry and sweating. He slapped his horse into the corral, replaced the pole gate and looked into the tackroom. Jimmy wasn't there, so he headed for the ranchhouse.

It took him about ten minutes to realize that the youngster had disappeared. Another ten minutes elapsed before he located Sam Harper who was clearing a spring of mud and stones on the sloping pasture to the east of the ranchhouse.

'You seen that boy?' Matt asked.

The greying ranchhand straightened. 'Ain't he foolin' around in that tackroom?'

'Nope. Ain't in the house, either.'

They went back together and it took them only a few more minutes to realize the boy had gone. A pony had been taken from the corral. A saddle and bridle were missing from the tackroom.

Matt Shayne moved swiftly and angrily to the house, a hunch drawing him to the rifle case in the living room. The glass front of the case had been forced open and the Winchester was gone, Matt Shayne went to the big oak cupboard where he kept his shells. A carton was missing.

He ran out of the building and stared grimly at the horizon beyond which lay Three Forks. Then he whipped around and glared at the skyline to the west, knowing that Caleb Dray's outfit was many miles across those ridges. Which direction had the boy taken? Which target had lured him on?

The missing gun irked Matt Shayne. What the devil had gotten into Jimmy? Maybe he had gone off on a jaunt and the gun was just incidental. Or maybe he had ideas of seeking revenge. Just who was the target? Caleb Dray, who had ordered his father to be hanged? Roper Stell? Stell had played a part in the lynching and had added to the boy's

70

hatred by putting him to work in his sweat shop.

Wiping perspiration from his face with his bandanna, Matt strode off to get his big horse. Moments later he was riding along the winding trail that skirted the mound of grassy hills that faced his ranch buildings. It was only a hunch that told him Jimmy had headed for Three Forks. Well, he'd soon see.

He was still within sight of the ranchhouse when a rifle cracked. The horse whinnied in pain and then his forelegs buckled. The animal rolled onto its side and Matt leaped clear and went into a roll. As he did, lead hissed through the air. He was moving, slithering, making himself a difficult target. The horse struggled to get up, making pitiful noises. Another burst of rifle fire spat bullets at the dry ground and he knew there was more than one gun. But still the slugs missed, some of them biting into the dust only inches from him. He slid out his Colt just as a voice shouted:

'You – Mr Stinking Shayne – we're gonna

get you this time!'

Walt Backus! Matt looked at the pitiful horse still kicking and trying to regain its feet, and fury shook every nerve in his body. Then he calmed as he heard the sound of boots dislodging stone and soil high up on the earthy mound. They were moving around him, taking cover in the thick scrub.

The ground rose behind him. A man could get above him. He had to move, maintain a position of height. There was a fold in the earth higher up the hill. It looked deep enough to hide a sheep – or a man. He ran. Then, as he dived for the fold, bullets sang after him. But he made the hollow and sank into it. Then he poked his Colt over a ledge and waited for a target. It came quickly enough as someone moved to change position. He fired twice. There was a yell from a male throat, but it was a cry of rage, not of pain.

Matt looked at the ridge above him. He would have to reach it before one of the others got there. Which meant another dangerous dash. He tensed, knowing the pain a slug inflicted. He had taken three in his lifetime, and the red scars were still vivid on his thigh and arm. Then he ran.

Shots tore at him the moment he plummeted from the hollow. He went through tearing scrub and dived for cover over the edge of the ridge, thankful he was still unbloodied. Then something told him there was a pursuer moving across the ridge. There was no time to huddle down; he turned. Walt Backus ran towards him.

Matt Shayne's gun barked and Walt Backus jerked back as if tugged by invisible ropes. By some miracle he kept his balance, but he swayed drunkenly. As agony flooded every other emotion from Walt Backus' brain he cried:

'Pa! Pa! He got me!'

Matt's gun arced around, but no one appeared. Then he heard the dying man fall to the ground and moan.

There was nothing pleasant about knowing you'd blasted the life from another human being. In fact, Matt trembled as his eyes scanned the scrub for another sign of movement.

But the other two were well hidden somewhere. There was one thing – Bill Backus knew he had lost another son. From somewhere among the earth, rocks and thornbush his enraged voice screamed hate. There was the girl's scream, too. And then a rifle pumped shell after futile shell at the earth ridge.

Matt Shayne kept his head well down. He knew he had the upper hand. If they rushed him he would kill another of them, maybe the girl, maybe her father. If they didn't rush, they'd live.

Matt held the heavy gun, felt the film of sweat under his palm. He could not hug this ridge forever. But maybe the other two would back down. It was a long way till sundown.

His intuition was right. Bill Backus was no longer young, but he had an animal's cunning. A creature of the wild always knew when to sink away. Although racked with anger, the oldster knew he couldn't rush a fast gunhand like Matt Shayne. He called to his daughter, 'Let's get. One day I'll kill him – but for now let's get. And you watch out, Liza.'

Matt heard the words and every nerve in his body relaxed. Then he heard the sounds made by boots on loose earth. They were retreating.

Judging simply by the tell-tale sounds, the young rancher knew he could move with comparative safety. They were climbing down the hillside; so he could beat a retreat and run for the safety of the ranch, taking cover most of the way.

He was scrambling along the safe side of the ridge, judging that the other two were somewhere among the brush and assessing their chances, when he saw a man walking out of the ranch yard. It was Sam Harper, gun in hand, obviously approaching to look into the shooting. He wasn't running; he was a wary man of fifty, dutiful but not impetuous.

Matt waited, standing on a convenient rock that overlooked the winding trail leading out of the T-Bar-T land. He held his Colt ready, but he had no intention of hunting for the other two. Let them lick their wounds...

But apparently Bill Backus had come up with a new idea – a wild, vengeful notion that suited him. Three horses suddenly thundered along the trail, one of them with an empty saddle. At full lope they charged in the direction of the ranch buildings. Crazed with anger, Bill Backus shouted.

'Burn the damn place down! Ride up, daughter – cover me – I'll fire some straw!'

Within seconds Backus and Liza were just about beneath the rock on which Matt stood. The impulse to act came without time for reflection. Bill Backus passed under the ledge first.

Matt Shayne dropped like an Apache onto the girl's horse. His arms went around her and she was pulled from the saddle. He fell on top of her and held her. The horse went on. Bill Backus hauled on the reins when he realized something was wrong, and he had to spend some valuable time in controlling the frightened horse. In that time Matt Shayne was able to control the girl's wild struggles. He gripped her savagely with one encircling arm and with his other hand he prodded her in the back with the Colt.

'Quit struggling! You want me to drill you?'

She froze. He rammed the hard weapon against her spine. He knew he couldn't shoot a woman in cold blood, but obviously the girl had doubts. She stopped fighting; only her heavy breathing showed the stress and anger within her. That and her hissed words: 'You mean snake! You're a killer, ain't you? First Red – and now Walt. Mister, I'm gonna drop you some day.'

'Pretty, ain't you?' Matt rasped. 'Like an animal. Now keep nice and still – your pa is trying to figure out what to do.'

Bill Backus, astride his mount, was slack-jawed, staring. Behind him, some two hundred yards down the trail, Sam Harper was walking slowly and carefully.

With a sudden surge of anger, Matt Shayne yelled at the trapper, 'I'm mighty tired of you, Backus – you and your family. I'll say it once again – Red died in a fair fight and he forced it on me. Walt died tryin' to kill me. Now you got the option to call it off right now. You can ride that nag right out of here – and keep away–'

'You gonna let Liza go?'

'That's the trick card, *hombre*. She can stay here and cool her heels until you see sense. Now get goin'.'

'What d'you aim to do with my gal? You can't keep her here.'

'I got an empty barn that says I can. So ride, feller. Just get away from here – and stay away. I'll let your daughter free in maybe two days – she should be cooled off by then – and even you might be seein' sense.'

'I'll get the law!' raged Bill Backus. 'You can't keep a gal locked up.'

'You can go get the law, Backus. Get Peake

out here and I'll tell him how you bush-whacked me.'

'You can't keep a gal locked up.' Bill Backus jerked a glance at the advancing Sam Harper. 'I know you no-good stinkin' polecats! What'll you do to her? She's a gal and you ain't particular.'

With sheer disgust and anger at this line of talk, Matt jerked the girl forward, the gun even more fiercely grinding against her spine. 'Get out of my way, Backus. She's going into that barn. You can haul away your dead son and give him a decent burial. If you want, get Peake out here – it'll give me a chance to tell him the truth. Now, are you movin'? Any gun trick will be your last.'

Almost speechless, unable to decide on a line of action, Bill Backus slowly jigged his horse down the trail. Then, seething with fury, he watched Matt Shayne force the girl along the rutted track towards the T-Bar-T buildings. He saw Matt meet Sam Harper and talk briefly, then the girl was pushed along.

Matt Shayne practically threw the girl into the barn. She stumbled and turned to face him, her dark eyes flashing. She was gunless, the weapon having been taken from her holster. Just as well. In her female fury she would have gone for the gun.

'I'll say it again,' she told Matt. 'I'll kill you, mister. You can't keep me here. My pa will get the sheriff for a start.'

'Cool off,' Matt said. 'You ain't going anywhere.'

5

Who Fired The Building?

The fire that raged in Three Forks gave the primitive fire brigade a real work-out. A human chain was formed and buckets of water were passed along and thrown onto the blazing shed that housed Roper Stell's manufacturing enterprises. The red glow coloured the night air, attracting men from the saloons, not all of whom helped. As long as the fire did not menace other property, some looked at it as a joke.

The water supply gave out and soon it was obvious that nothing would save the tinder-dry shed.

Sheriff Phil Peake was among the men trying to keep the fire from spreading to adjoining buildings. Roper Stell grabbed his arm.

'Sheriff, some dastardly swine has started this fire! I checked the place myself last thing after Novak went away.'

'You can't be sure,' Peake said. 'You had a forge in this building. Maybe some sparks flew off.'

'That forge is surrounded by firebrick,' yelled the small man. 'It was no accident, Sheriff. The place just roared into a blaze. I was at my home when I was told – and I'd just left the shed ten minutes afore that. Novak and my other men had gone, and the two boys were in their bunks.'

'They're safe, I guess? Where are they now?'

'I don't know. They ran off, damn them! Say, maybe *they* started the fire.'

'Why should they?'

'Well, they dislike me because I'm their master. But I thought they were afraid of me.'

'Scared outa their little miserable lives, I should have thought,' said Phil Peake drily.

Roper Stell shook two bony fists at the remains of his shed. 'Some rat has ruined me!'

'You ain't lost for ready cash,' said Phil Peake. 'That's in the bank, I take it.'

'You have little sympathy in my loss, Sheriff.'

'I'm a bit hot and sweaty, I guess.'

'You didn't take action against Shayne, I note.'

'When the judge hits town.'

'That boy!' Roper Stell began to dance with rage. 'It could be that boy!'

'He's miles away, on the T-Bar-T.'

The sheriff edged away from Roper Stell. He'd had enough of the little man. The walking skeleton irked him, got on his nerves. Still, Roper Stell was influential, a voice on the committee. An insistent voice.

There was one man on the fringe of the crowd who had a mind full of doubts and worries. He sat his horse, a fresh mount from the T-Bar-T.

Matt Shayne had left his ranch after the

girl had been secured for the evening. He'd ridden carefully, fearing an ambush by Bill Backus, but it didn't materialize. He'd entered town just as the sun sank behind the distant mountains. He was searching for sign of Jimmy Skinner when the red glow attracted him. Now, looking at the ruins of the shed, he asked himself the obvious question: Had Jimmy done this?

The thought was given more impact when he overheard fragments of loud talk between two men. 'Stell says some gent fired the place...'

'I ain't surprised – he made plenty of enemies.'

'Could've been them lads he's got indentured...'

'Fancy talk,' sneered the other. 'He works them young-uns into the ground. Sometimes they don't even get wages.'

Matt Shayne wheeled his horse around and almost ran down Phil Peake. The big man grasped the horse's leathers.

'Howdy, Shayne! You smell fire all them

miles back along the trail?'

'Nope.'

'What brings you into town again?'

'Waal, for a start, I want to file a complaint against the Backus crew. They came gunnin' for me at my spread. Walt got himself killed.'

Phil Peake pushed his hat back. 'You killed the other son, too?'

'My man Sam Harper will act as my witness. It was self-defence.'

'He's your man.'

'I got two hands. The other, Manuel Reyna, heard the shooting even if he didn't see what was goin' on. You're welcome to make any check you figure should be made.'

'Where's the body?'

'I think the father took it away.'

'If hate could kill, you should be dead.' Phil Peake stared back at the crowd and the dying blaze. 'What about the girl? She's a real mean one. She'll–'

'She tried to gun me, along with her pa and brother. I've got her locked in a barn. She can go hungry and beat her grubby

85

hands against the walls. She needs to be taught a lesson.'

The lawman stroked his luxuriant moustache. 'You got any ideas about this fire, Shayne?'

Matt shrugged. 'They worked with fire in that joint, didn't they?'

'Stell is bawlin' that it was started deliberately. Means I'll have to take a real close look at the whole thing. That boy is safe and sound at the T-Bar-T, I take it?'

Matt returned the lawman's narrow-eyed stare with a blank look. 'Sure. He likes the ranch, and you know as well as I do that Stell has no real claim on him.'

'That ain't in the clear yet,' snapped Phil Peake. 'If that skinny galoot can persuade the judge to make an order tellin' you to hand him over, you've lost out.'

Matt edged his horse away. He wanted to avoid more talk with the lawman because even a hedged question about Jimmy Skinner could make the man suspicious. In truth, he wasn't sure that the boy had headed for Three Forks. He could be Indian-footing around Caleb Dray's place with some idea of vengeance. Or maybe he had returned to the T-Bar-T after a few hours of pot-shooting anything that moved in the hills around the ranch.

Matt rode around the town for awhile, finally hitching his mount to the rail outside The Splendide. He had no aim in mind other than a few words with Violet Denton. She wouldn't know a thing about the boy, but he wanted to talk, to be near her.

She entered the hotel lounge like a goddess, her flowing dress glinting with sequins and clinging to her full figure. She held out her hand to Matt. He thought she expected him to kiss it; she was that kind of woman. Amused, he held the hand and that was all.

'How nice to see you again, Matt.' She looked at the bruise on his face, the cuts and scratches on the backs of his hands. 'I hear you've been in the wars again with those Backus people and that dumb brute, Novak.'

'You hear plenty.'

'And you've got a boy with you – young Skinner. You'd better watch him, Matt.'

'I can handle him. How about a drink, Violet?'

They sat in a dim corner on a red plush settee made for two. A negro waiter brought drinks. Matt relaxed and began to talk.

'Oh, dear, you do get involved,' Violet said when he'd told her about Jimmy. 'You shouldn't be so concerned...'

'They hanged his father.' Matt said grimly.

'But he was no good. He was destined for a violent death. Oh, Matt, do watch that boy.'

'Now don't worry,' he said easily. 'He's just a kid. He just needs someone to tell him right from wrong.'

'He'll never know that. He's got bad blood. It tells. It's bred in him.'

He stared. 'What's bred in him, Violet?'

'Oh, you know ... thieving ... lying ... the instinct to kill...'

'Haven't we all got the same instincts?'

88

'Good heavens, no! Really, Matt, you're a gentleman – you know the difference.'

'I've killed men.'

'Defending yourself. Or for a just cause – like a soldier might do in the line of duty. You have good instincts, Matt. You're an honourable man. Why, we wouldn't be such good friends if I didn't know that.' Her hand sought his.

He looked around the softly-lit lounge; at the carpet, the expensive wallpaper. The odour of good food came faintly from the rear. Yes, the murderers, the haters, the dirt – that was all outside and Violet would keep it there.

'I thought you'd understand about Jimmy Skinner,' he said. 'He's just a kid.'

'Forget him, Matt,' she said earnestly. 'Put him out. Give him to Roper Stell. He'll really teach him something.'

'Yeah, to hate even worse.' He downed his drink. 'I think I ought to go, Violet. Back to the ranch.'

'You could stay here.' Her wide blue eyes

were warm with an invitation. 'It's a long ride back, Matt. Please stay. And forget about that Skinner boy.'

She was soft, gentle, beautiful. He was about to accept her invitation when she said:

'Mick Skinner was a loser because he was born bad. I heard about him. He robbed a friend of mine – a gentleman of means. And that boy must be rotten. Caleb Dray did the right thing stringing up the father – it's one way to teach the brat a lesson–'

'He's a boy of twelve,' protested Matt. His eyes roamed around the expensive furnishings of the hotel. A wealthy rancher took his ease in a padded chair; a drummer in an immaculate new suit in another corner, viewed his wine glass with approval. 'You've got it made, Violet – and you don't want to know about anything else…'

'It wasn't always like this,' she said sharply.

'I know.' He rose. 'Thanks for the drink, Violet. I think I'd better go after all.'

She watched him leave and he didn't see

the disappointment sparking in her blue, blue eyes.

It was a long ride back home and he couldn't hurry the tired horse. He was full of angry thoughts when he finally reached the ranch yard and saw a gleam of yellow light. Maybe Sam Harper had lit the log fire and left the lamp burning, knowing he might be home that night. Maybe there would be news of Jimmy. As for the Backus girl, he'd throw her out tomorrow.

As Matt rode into the ranch yard the door of the bunkhouse opened and Sam Harper came out to take the horse. 'I'll see to him, boss. The boy is back, by the way – and that hell-cat nearly tore down your barn.'

Matt went into the house with slow strides, knocking trail dust from his vest and pants with his hat. Inside the wide, log-walled room with its huge stone fireplace stood Jimmy, grinning warily at him.

Matt kept his temper. He noted the scruffy state of the boy's jeans and shirt. There was yellow earth sticking to his shoes

– moist earth. Matt swung to the rifle case. The Winchester was back in place. He walked over. There was no need to find the key; the glass-fronted door had been forced. He took the Winchester out and examined it. 'You've been using this gun.'

'Sure,' Jimmy said. 'I used it...'

'What on?'

'I went huntin'.'

'Did you think about asking permission first? Did it cross your mind that I'd wonder where you'd gone?'

'Aw, I just got the idea and went. I got sick of that tackroom.'

'You didn't by any chance ride as far as Three Forks?'

The boy blinked. 'Well, I got there and then I looked around. You're gonna hit me, ain't you?'

'I'd pick on some galoot my own size if I wanted to hit somebody. Why'd you go to town?'

'I told you – I just wanted to sashay around.'

'Were you thinkin' about Roper Stell?'

'Yeah, a bit,' he said defiantly. 'I hate him. He strung up my pa – him and that dirty big rancher, Caleb Dray.'

'You can't forget, can you?'

'Would you?' the lad suddenly shouted. 'I saw my pa danglin'. He – he yelled for help, but they didn't stop. He yelled...'

Matt drew in a deep breath. 'Did you set fire to Roper Stell's barn?' In spite of his desire to be sympathetic, he rapped out the question.

Jimmy Skinner flared instantly at the accusation. A jeer settled on his thin face. 'So that's it! That's where you've been! Ridin' around. So some gink set fire to the mucky place, eh? Good! Well, maybe it was me! I sure wish I'd done it. Maybe I did. You don't know for sure, do you, mister? Yeah, maybe I did set fire to the place. Me, I'm a liar, ain't I? You don't know for sure what's the truth.'

'Now, look, Jimmy – you run away, you take a horse and gun without permission, and you say you've been to Three Forks.'

'Sure, I set fire to the place!' Jimmy shouted suddenly. 'I'm bad enough, ain't I? And I'd've killed Stell for sure if I'd seen him! You'd better lock up them guns, mister. Maybe you'd better lock me up, too, 'cause I'm gonna hit back for what they did to my pa. I've been foolin' around long enough. I've got a big list – that Dray feller – the two stinkin' ranch hands that held me – and Stell. You think I'd forget what they did to my pa? You really figure that?'

Matt Shayne turned around and swallowed his temper. When he looked at the boy some moments later, his face was calm. 'I'll talk to you in the morning. Better get some sleep, boy – you might need it. If people saw you in Three Forks last night and they talk to the law about it, you could be in trouble.'

'How do you know I won't run away tonight?'

'You came back here.'

'I was hungry.'

'And you're tired and need sleep – so

94

you'll stay.' Matt Shayne unbuckled his gunbelt. 'Come sunup, you'll want to talk sense to me, Jimmy – or I miss my guess.'

6

Garriga – The Hunter

Matt decided to take breakfast to the Backus girl himself. He doubted if her temper would be any better. Anyway, she could leave as soon as she liked. She could walk back to Three Forks; it would do her good.

She nearly threw the plate at him. Only the sight of the sizzling bacon, three eggs and fried bread changed her mind. Then she stared at the pot of coffee and she licked her lips. But her dark eyes held a murderous glint.

For a moment, Matt Shayne was taken aback by the pure venom in her look. Then he realized he had killed two of her brothers.

Stung to words, he said defensively, 'They went for me. First it was Red – with his taunts, his open invitation in front of a crowd to go for a gun. Then Walt – he'd've killed me, you know that.'

'I'll kill you some day,' she flung at him.

Drawing on all his patience, he said, 'Better call it off. Go tell your father to light out for the hills where you two belong. You can only get me by a bushwhack – and I'll be careful how I travel from now on. You two couldn't draw down on me. I've tangled with the best.'

She picked up some bacon with her fingers and stuffed it into her mouth. There was a fork at the side of the plate. 'I'm gonna kill you, mister.' She spat out each word. 'I'm a Backus. I hate real good. And I sure hate you.'

He turned and walked to the open door, where he paused to say, 'You can go just when you like. But remember you'll be watched.'

'I could set fire to this place,' she said.

'I've thought of that – so you'd better walk real fast when you leave.'

She scooped the rest of the food into her mouth with the fork, then threw the plate at him. He dodged it and she wiped her hands down her dark jeans. Then she tucked her long dark hair under her battered hat. 'My gun?' she said.

'Let's go get it.'

Eyes glittering, she followed him to the living room. She looked around. 'My, my! Home sweet home, Mr Shayne. Well, make the most of it – you ain't got long to live.'

He was handing her the empty handgun, his resentment mounting, when she snatched the weapon and tried to hit him with it. His hand closed on her wrist with the lightning speed for which he was known. She struggled. He got an arm around her and drew her closer to him. There was nothing gentle about his grip; he nearly broke her arm as he held her gunhand. She fought like a wildcat, clawing at his eyes. He rammed down the hand. Her oval face was close to his jutting jaw. As they battled, he was crazily aware of her roundness, of the fact that she was, after all, a woman. His thoughts angered him.

'You're a she-cat!' he snarled. 'You ain't really a woman – you're a pesky varmint. Somebody should larrup you.'

She spat in his face. He flung her from him. She staggered to the door and tripped on the Indian rug, ending up in a sitting position. She glared up at him.

'I'll gun you down, Mr Rancher – see if I don't.' She got up, scrambled for her gun and then backed to the door. 'I'm killin' you – remember that!'

In the next instant, she slipped away like a lithe creature of the wilderness. Matt Shayne sucked in his breath, his thoughts churning. Then he saw Jimmy Skinner standing in the doorway leading from his bedroom.

'That's the Backus gal,' the boy said. 'The one that wanted to see you dead. She sure kicked up a rumpus last night afore you came home.'

'Yeah. They came gunnin' for me. Walt stopped a slug...'

'Her other brother?'

'Yep, boy. He figured a gun was the only way to settle things: He was right, in a way, because he's dead.'

Jimmy nodded, then he said gravely, 'I got to talk to you, Mr Shayne, about last night.'

'Go ahead, kid.'

'I did go to Three Forks. Then I–'

At that moment an interruption came in the shape of a shout from Sam Harper in the yard:

'Mr Shayne, you've got visitors.'

When Matt went outside there were three riders in the yard. Sam Harper and Manuel Reyna were staring blankly at them. One rider was Sheriff Phil Peake, looking disgruntled.

Another was Roper Stell, sitting his saddle like a bird of prey, his dark suit too large for him.

'There's the boy,' Stell said. 'Grab the

young brute!'

'Hold it, Stell.' Phil Peake's lips barely moved under his thick moustache.

Matt's gaze went to the third man who was on a big chestnut. His leering, calculating smile went to Matt, assessing what he saw. Bunt Garriga was a big man. He wore a thick leather vest and a three-inch-wide gunbelt. His ammunition belt glinted in the morning sun.

There was a passenger on the back of the big horse. Liza Backus rode behind the gunslinger. Her red lips were parted in a triumphant smile.

'He fired my place last night.' Roper Stell's bony finger pointed at Jimmy Skinner. 'He did it! He was seen in town last night! Arrest him, Peake – do I need to tell you any more?'

'I don't need to hear another word,' said Peake heavily, 'but maybe Shayne would like to hear the charge – I've been hearin' it for the past ten miles.'

'This boy set fire to my premises last night!' shrilled Roper Stell. 'He was seen on the streets in Three Forks. I've got two witnesses who will swear to that. A lot of folks know he's a venomous little devil – he even attacked my man Novak. Do I need to say any more, Peake?'

The sheriff looked straight at Matt. 'It's your say. Where was the boy last night?'

Matt thinned his lips and didn't answer. Sam Harper exchanged a glance with Manuel Reyna. Liza Backus laughed thinly.

'Well?' Sheriff Peake eased his rump in the saddle. There was nothing about this that pleased him. He didn't like any of the company – and that included Matt Shayne.

'You were in town, Shayne. We talked. You told me Jimmy Skinner was here on this ranch.'

'I don't know where the boy was last night when the shed caught fire,' said Matt, 'because I wasn't here at the ranch to swear to it.'

'That ain't an answer,' said the lawman. 'Was this kid here or not?'

Matt Shayne was saved from having to

find an answer as the boy's voice rang out jeeringly:

'Sure, I was in town last night. I got back just ahead of Mr Shayne. I took a horse and a gun – and if I'd seen that dirty little killer over there, I'd've shot him dead.' Jimmy Skinner pointed to Roper Stell.

'What more do you want?' screamed the little man. 'He tried to ruin me! And after I extended a helping hand!'

Matt turned to the boy. 'What the devil are you trying to do to yourself? You–'

'They hung my pa! I saw him dyin'! You want me to say "yes, please" to everybody? You think I should be glad of a bed and some grub? Nobody ain't doin' a thing about Stell – or that big, fat rancher, Caleb Dray. But I aim to! Yes, sir! I'll kill 'em. I'm a Skinner – ain't that right? I'm real bad.'

Matt laid a hand on the boy's shoulder and gripped him hard. 'You're talking wild again. You were all set to tell me something when these fellers arrived. Now what was it?'

The boy struggled against Matt's restraining hand. 'Lemme go! I ain't sayin' anything – except that you'll have to kill me if you want to stop me hatin'.'

'I've heard enough,' snapped the sheriff. 'Hold him, Shayne. He's coming back with us. I'll put him in a cell.'

'A boy? In jail?'

'I've had young hellions before.' Peake got down from his saddle. 'He'll cool off. Hell, he's dangerous.'

'What do you figure to do with him?' Matt kept his protective arm around the boy.

'He should have been hanged with his miserable father!' raged Roper Stell.

'Judge Burch will deal with him.' Peake lurched over to Matt. 'I guess he'll be sent to a home.'

'Most of them are pretty grim, judging by what I've heard,' Matt said.

'A hard life never hurt nobody,' said the lawman. 'Spare the rod and spoil the child – you know that. Look at this young menace. He don't know a damn thing about discipline.'

'He could learn.'

'Yep. He'll do just that, I guess – in a home. If he don't toe the line there, he'll be black and blue for weeks. I guess he'll learn.'

'Yeah, to hate even more,' Matt muttered.

The sheriff placed a firm hand on Jimmy's shoulder. 'You're coming along with us, Skinner. You can make a statement to the judge – and it had better be the truth because Judge Burch is not a man to fool with.'

There was a struggle with the boy and Peake had to tie his wrists together with a short length of rope.

Matt Shayne watched while Jimmy was hoisted to the sheriff's saddle and the lawman got ready to mount. He came to a quick decision. 'I'm riding in with you.'

'We can deal with him,' returned Peake.

'I trust you, Sheriff, but not the others.'

'You can please yourself,' declared Phil Peake. 'This is still a free country. You ride along if you want.'

'Watch him, Sheriff,' Liza Backus suddenly

cried. 'He's a killer! You oughta have him behind bars.'

'You'd do well to hold your tongue,' barked Peake. 'I ain't too pleased with you and your loco bunch.'

The fleshy face of Bunt Garriga creased in a leer. 'Gunhand turned cowman! Maybe it's because he don't like bein' drawn on any more.'

Matt turned to Sam Harper. 'Look after things, will you? And you, too, Manuel.'

The two men nodded. 'Don't worry about anything here,' added Manuel Reyna.

It was a slow ride back to Three Forks, with Matt tagging along in the rear, watching the others. Bunt Garriga turned frequently to flash his fleshy smile, and Liza Backus flung some taunts, stopping only when Peake growled at her to shut up. Jimmy Skinner sat bright-eyed and tight-lipped. Once Matt rode up and tried to speak to him, but the boy kept a stony silence.

In this way they left the valley and headed across the wide rangeland. In the distance the Pecos River wound like a blue snake. To the east, near the tributary, the up-and-coming town of Three Forks was sprawled.

Jimmy was placed in a cell. Matt stood at the bars and said, 'I'm your friend, Jimmy. Just remember that. If you've got anything to say, tell me now.'

'You wouldn't believe me.'

'I might.'

'Folks will say you're crazy,' jeered the boy. 'Just imagine anybody believin' a Skinner. I got nothin' to say.'

Matt decided to return later to the sheriff's office. Maybe he would stay in town until Judge Burch returned; a word with the man might be helpful.

Roper Stell had disappeared, his eyes glittering and resentful. He had taken his man with him.

And Liza Backus had slid from the rump of the big chestnut without warning and had run into a side street. There was a reason. She had glimpsed her father waving urgently from the shadow of a livery door.

Bill Backus grasped Liza's arm and sat her on a bale of straw. 'That damned gunny – didn't you get a chance to kill him?'

'I was locked in a barn,' she flared.

His grimy face twisted. 'Girl, you could've done him in with a knife or a hammer – anythin'.'

'I didn't get the chance, Pa.'

'What were they doin' riding in like that?'

'It's that Skinner brat. Seems like he set fire to that iron-workin' shed on the other side of town. They're sticking him in the jail.' She paused. 'Do we get even with Shayne? We ain't finished, are we?'

'With two sons dead?' He shook his big head. 'I won't rest until we spill his blood in the dust.'

She stared down at the ground. 'Poor Walt … and Red. Maybe we did fight at times, but they were good to me … sometimes. I just remember…' Her voice trailed off and she sat staring, rocking slightly.

'We'll get him tonight,' Bill Backus said. 'With two guns on him, he can't win.'

Matt Shayne tried to relax when Violet Denton walked into the hotel lounge. She looked fresh and lovely in an expensive calico dress that had been made back East, he guessed. The emerald colour suited her. She greeted him with a kiss, putting cool lips to his cheek and then stepping back to look searchingly at him.

'My, you do look like a cowhand,' she said.

He nodded. 'I could do with a drink.' He hesitated. 'But maybe you've got more presentable company? Like some of the gents who come here with their fine suits and clean boots?'

'You'd outdo all of them in a new serge suit, Matt, my man.'

He smiled bitterly. 'As long as I could wear a gunbelt with it...'

He stayed in the hotel all that day and got a bit drunk. He'd have to wait for Judge Burch to get to town, and it seemed he was expected on the stage tomorrow afternoon.

He could, of course, just wash his hands of

Jimmy Skinner. After all, the boy wasn't his kin. And he had ranch work to do. Also, he had enemies. But Matt knew he was stuck with the problem of Jimmy Skinner. For some reason he just couldn't drop the boy.

There was a card game going in the hotel. He joined it but had little luck. He threw in his cards and went to the bar. Then Violet Denton joined him again and they talked of many things. But he got the impression she was skimming over details of her past. And when two painted ladies guided two gentlemen up the wide, ornate stairs to the hotel bedrooms, he knew why he had reservations about Violet.

Feeling restless, he told her, 'I'll take a walk.'

'Are you tired of my company?'

He grinned at her, touched her bare arm. 'I just think I've had too much of your fine whiskey.'

'Mind how you go. And be back here before midnight – we run a respectable establishment–'

He grinned wider at that. Minutes later he was walking slowly along the boardwalk of the main street. He wondered if he should pay a visit to the sheriff's office or maybe look in The Big Chance saloon. In range garb, gunbelt and hardware, he'd be more suited to the saloon than the classy hotel. But he wasn't sure. Maybe he'd just take the night air and think about tomorrow while he cleared his brain of whiskey fumes.

Instincts born of danger told him that someone was following him. He didn't hurry. He didn't even turn. His ears were tuned to every sound in the night.

For some moments he trudged along slowly, taking in the odd noises that warned him. The swift tap-tap of feet, then a pause – he heard the pattern again. Two punchers came down the planks, arguing about something. He let them pass, turning slightly, his narrowed eyes searching for movement. Nothing. He moved on. Another five yards and light from The Big Chance spilled over the boardwalk and road, a yellow pool that made the surrounding darkness even thicker.

Obeying an impulse, he turned quickly and went through the batwings. Inside the place, he looked around for a point of concealment. The place was fairly crowded, but no one seemed to notice him. Seeing a small barricade of stacked tables – extras for busy nights – he slid behind them and waited. He could be wrong, but maybe he'd soon know who'd been following him.

He smiled in satisfaction when the big shape of the man whom Stell had addressed as Bunt Garriga walked through the batwings and stood there, looking, searching. His large hands hovered over his twin Colts. The wide yellow gunbelt was new. The guns looked heavy. Two-gun men were few and far between, Matt knew, and in some cases their skill was dubious. But Garriga's hands relaxed. One went to his hat and tilted it. Then, turning, he went out.

Matt walked forward and waited near the batwings. Garriga was Stell's hireling. He'd followed him – and it wasn't to shake his hand.

Why the devil did a man like Roper Stell hate so much? True, he'd been humiliated by Matt, and he'd been thwarted in his plans for Jimmy Skinner. Evidently he'd hated the boy's father sufficiently to join a necktie party. Maybe Skinner senior had robbed him. But Roper Stell's hate was the kind that would engulf him. He was destroying himself. Hiring Garriga was a further move in that direction.

Matt Shayne walked slowly into the night and moved away from the pool of yellow light. From across the road a voice said:

'Hello, Mr Shayne.'

7

Another Dead Man

It was Garriga's voice. His bulk was a dark shape on the boardwalk.

Matt froze, hands clear of his sides. 'What do you want?'

'You know.' There was a gloating in the other man's voice that Matt recognized; he'd heard it often before.

'You calling me?' Matt asked.

'Could be.'

'Any time,' Matt said.

There was a pause. One man was already dead. He just had to fall.

Matt Shayne sensed the fleeting seconds more than he counted them – and then he saw the man with the two guns claw for his weapons.

Matt drew and fired. Then Garriga's big guns went off and the slugs whined viciously. But only one bullet found a target: Bunt Garriga's heart. The other two bullets had been fired just as the slug from Matt's gun thumped into Garriga, and the death-dealing bits of metal went off-course.

Garriga staggered back and dropped his guns. He leaned against the brick wall, then slowly he sank, a hand grasping his shirt where blood pumped from a heart that was pounding to its final spasm. Matt Shayne, frozen, gun still pointed, watched Garriga fall limply, feeling empty.

Men had heard the shots and now they came out of the saloon. Some darted across the street to the huddled form on the boardwalk. 'It's Garriga.'

Matt holstered his gun and walked away. Only one place offered a refuge to him and that was Violet's hotel, The Splendide. But he was stopped by the sheriff.

'Where the devil do you figure you're going?'

'To see Violet Denton. Get outa my way…'

'I warned you,' Phil Peake growled. 'You gunslinging bastard! You've killed three men from this town. I told you this was a peaceful place. I won't have gunnies around.'

'He called me out,' Matt said. 'What the devil would you have me do?'

'You were called out because you've got a rep. If you weren't here, it wouldn't have happened. We had only one shoot-up in twelve months in this town, and now you–'

'You also had a lynch party. You weren't so het-up about that.'

A big figure emerged from the glowing light of a hotel. It was Caleb Dray, elbowing belligerently forward.

'You, Shayne, again…' Dray was immaculate in a grey suit. His head was bare and his regular-featured face was set gravely. 'I've been hearing about you.'

'I take it you didn't like what you heard,' Matt said.

'You've been siding with that Skinner brat.

And you couldn't control him – look at what he did to Stell's factory. In a way, you're responsible for that. You gave him the idea he could challenge Stell – not that he really needed any encouragement.'

'You'll be happy that the boy's in jail,' Matt snapped.

'Best place for him until he can be sent to a home.'

Matt nodded. 'Best place – seein' that he's threatened to kill you for stringing up his father. If I were you, Dray, I wouldn't sleep so good at night.'

The glare that came from the big rancher's eyes told Matt Shayne that he had made another enemy.

Then Phil Peake came striding back after a fast inspection of the body. 'Another hit at Stell! He had this man on hire.'

'For what?' Matt asked.

'General work – a bodyguard,' blustered Phil Peake.

'He figured he was a gunslinger because he toted two guns,' came Matt's curt reply.

'I suggest that you talk to Roper Stell about employing gunmen in a town which you state is peaceful.'

'Now look here, Shayne—'

'You all through, gentlemen?' Matt directed a glance at the lawman and Caleb Dray. 'I'm going to The Splendide for the night.' He stabbed a finger at Peake's chest. 'Seein' you're so all-fired concerned, maybe you'll tell Roper Stell that I don't like bein' set up for target practice.'

'It wouldn't have happened if you weren't here!' roared the sheriff.

There was an element of truth in that, and Matt had to nod. Then he returned to the hotel and had a stiff drink. He was staring into the smouldering embers of the log fire in the lounge when Violet Denton came to him and placed a hand on his arm. 'I've heard about the shooting. Oh, Matt, you've made so many enemies.'

'Yeah, and three of them are dead. I guess it's only a matter of elimination before folks leave me alone.'

'I won't leave you alone...'

'Thanks, Violet, but right now I'm not good company. I'm going to bed. I'm tired – or is it the whiskey?'

'My room is very comfortable,' she whispered. 'And private...'

He didn't know why he had to push away the temptation. Violet was a desirable woman, but he couldn't stop thinking about the long line of men she had undoubtedly known. He was no Sunday School teacher himself. He had spent money on saloon girls – and had regretted it the next day for some loco reason. So he was rebuffing Violet for little reason. But it was there – the mental picture of a long line of men, with himself at the end of the queue.

Mumbling an excuse, he left her. This time the glint in her blue eyes was hard and bitter.

He locked his hotel room door and placed a chair under the knob. He took off his vest and shirt, went to the wash-stand and poured cold water from the large china jug.

He found soap and washed his head and face, then his chest. He then slung his gunbelt and Colt over the bed post, got out of his tight pants and, wearing only long johns, slid under the bedclothes. He lay there, thinking.

Maybe he should ride out to his ranch in the morning and say the hell with Three Forks. He had a rep and he was getting in bed with everybody.

Was it worth bothering with Jimmy Skinner? Hell, did he owe the boy anything? Maybe he was hell-bent and would follow his father's steps to a bad end no matter what happened.

As these thoughts ran through his mind, two shadowy figures on the other side of the road stared at the lights of The Splendide. The man and woman stood close together, watching with resentful eyes.

'He's in there,' grated Bill Backus.

'I saw him tug the drapes,' agreed the girl. 'That's his room.' And she pointed up at the façade of the hotel. 'There's a lamp burnin'.

121

You figure he's gone to sleep?'

'Give the killer a bit of time, gal. Sure, he'll be in bed. See that balcony around them windows? I reckon you could climb up there and get to that window real easy. You could do for that killer, gal.'

'Me? Ain't you gonna give me a hand, Pa?'

'I can't climb so good at my age. But you can shinny up … get a grip on them balcony rails … and I figure that window of his is open. Real convenient, ain't it?'

'He killed another man tonight,' she said. 'That big hellion I rode back with.'

'I know, gal. Don't the whole town know it? All the better – ain't nobody gonna fret if they find him with a knife in him. You got that knife handy, girl.'

'Yes.'

'You know how to use it?'

'I've gutted a few bears in my time…'

'Ain't no real difference,' he sneered. 'Man or bear – they got a belly.'

She nodded. Some men passed on the other side of the street. A moment later a one-horse gig drew up at the front of the hotel. Down the street, a lone rider hunched in a sheepskin coat, allowed his horse to plod on. When there was a quiet moment, Bill Backus touched his daughter's arm. 'All right – let's get. I'll give you a lift up to that balcony, girl.'

They walked over. A minute later, Liza drew herself up to the ornamental rail that ran around the balcony on the first floor. Bill Backus gave a chuckle and darted back across the road, hugging the darkness. He watched the slight figure crawl along the balcony. There was one good thing about a knife – it made no noise. And when Matt Shayne lay gutted, his sons would be avenged.

She got to the window. Impelled by primitive urges, she felt that killing this man would be the solution to her hate. With him dead, her mind could be clear again. It wouldn't bring Walt and Red back to life, but there'd be satisfaction and she could go back to the hills with her father and resume their life of trapping and killing for fur. He had to die. He deserved to die. And she would squeal with delight when she did it.

She was able to raise the window and slide through without making a sound. She stood in the small room, noting with swift eyes the man asleep in the bed, the door with the chair rammed under the knob, the gunbelt hooked over the brass post.

She felt triumph as she drew the Bowie knife and eyed the figure on the bed. His breathing came to her ears and she was sure he was sound asleep.

This tall devil with the lean face was hers to hack and destroy. The very thought of it excited her. She felt her heart beat more rapidly. She could leap at him ... or creep like an Apache. She decided on the latter.

She moved quietly. There was no tinge of fear, no feeling of doubt or conscience – until the last moment, when she saw the hawk-like cut of nose and jaw. She stared for a long time at his face, seeing the firm lips, the lean cheeks.

This was the man who had killed her brothers. But somehow he looked different, lying there so motionless. He didn't seem to be the same man she had struggled with back at the T-Bar-T. She'd loathed him when he'd tried to subdue her; she still hated him, but it was queer how peaceful he looked, just lying there. And there was something good-looking about the rest of his face.

Her hand went up. The knife glinted in the light from the lamp on the chest of drawers.

The sense of movement in the still room sent an urgent signal to some nerve in Matt Shayne's head. He rolled to the side and the knife plunged down and sliced into the pillow. Matt was jerking frantically, twisting around. He saw the glittering dark eyes, the long black hair in disarray under the battered hat as she raised the knife again. But her wrist was in his hand before she could stab down. Then both wrists were claimed and her hand slid away from the knife handle. Another heave and she fell back across the lower part of the bed. Matt

Shayne pressed down on her. She fell to the floor and he held her down, arms spread wide. His eyes glared at her. Now she saw nothing but savagery in his face; gone was the look of peace. The black hairs on his chest caught her eyes and the impression of masculinity was an utterly crazy thought at a time when she was struggling with him. She had to get free. The knife – if only she could reach it! She wasn't done yet!

After some minutes of struggling with him, however, she knew that her chance of killing him had gone. She couldn't reach the knife and she couldn't get free. Finally, gasping for breath, she lay back, spent.

'I should throw you out the window,' grated Matt Shayne.

'I'll kill you some day,' she muttered.

'What are you, an animal? Ain't you a woman?'

Her reply was a scream of hate. 'Two brothers I had – and you shot them down. I'll never forget that!'

Suddenly his old curiosity about this girl

returned. He saw the oval face, the flashing eyes in the faint light from the lamp. Surely, behind her anger and bitterness was a different person. Fumbling for words, hardly knowing why he bothered to talk, he said, 'Why the hell don't you clean yourself up? Why don't you get that damned hair washed? Why don't you wear a dress?'

They were crazy questions. He hadn't meant to ask them. Why should he even wonder about this girl? She was a primitive hill creature, brought up to gut and skin animals.

He got answers spat back at him. Curses. Insults. He heaved her to a sitting position. He noted the movement of her full breasts under the black shirt.

'Who told you to ape your dirty brothers?' he asked. 'Who brought you up? Your father? Did you ever know your mother?'

'I had a good mother,' she said, almost gently. Then the bitterness returned. 'But I ain't bandying fancy words with you.'

'No? Well, we got plenty of time. You came

to kill me – you can talk instead.'

She flashed him a savage look. 'You ain't even dressed.'

'Long johns,' he said calmly. 'You must have seen a man in long johns afore – your pa, your brothers...'

'That was different...'

'You want me to put on pants?'

'Yeah.'

He released her arms and walked to his pants, turning his back to her.

She grabbed at the heavy water jug that stood on the wash-stand and swung it at him. But he knew she was moving and he had expected her reaction the moment he turned his back. He was testing her. She didn't know that.

He caught the heavy jug as it moved through the air and deftly took it from her. Water splashed over the two of them. As he whipped the jug away, she fought to hold it and stood off-balance. He gave her a kick with a stockinged foot that sent her reeling back.

When he had turned again, the jug on the floor, he had hold of his pants. But he didn't try to climb into them. He thought with a trace of grim humour that a man trying to climb into tight pants was in a vulnerable position for at least half a minute.

'I was trying to get some sleep when you crept in here like a skunk,' he said. 'You weren't invited, but you can stay.'

'What do you mean?' Facing him, her girlish figure in a crouch, she showed fear for the first time.

'I'll show you.' He was on her in a flash. He forced her down to a chair as if she was a calf being thrown. Working with brutal strength, he tugged the bandanna from around her throat and used it to tie her hands. In a corner of the bedroom some thin drapes were used to form a sort of closet. He tore down the material and ripped it into long lengths. He bound the girl to the chair, pulling the bindings tightly around her waist. Once again he noticed the female shape under the dirty male garb and the smile left his face. He bound her ankles to the seat in the same manner. There was plenty of the cotton material. He paused. 'I've got some fool ideas for you, my girl. Seein' you crept in, you can stay. Tomorrow you can ride out with me to a place I know where they might be able to turn you into a woman. Maybe then you'll quit thinking of trying to kill me.'

'You can't keep me here – I'll yell.'

'Then you'll wear a gag.'

'My Pa...'

Matt Shayne nodded. 'He's somewhere outside waitin' for you. I guessed that. Well, he can chew his dirty fingers off wondering just what's happened to you.'

'What do you figure to do with me? What do you mean by fool ideas?'

It was her last cry because he began to wrap the cotton cloth around her mouth. He said, 'Don't worry about your body. You'd need to be put in sheep-dip before I'd touch you – if that's what you've been thinking. Nope, I just got an idea. If I can't get rid of you by killing you, then there's only one way to deal with you. You've got to change. I'll put you somewheres where your pa can't reach you, among folks who will teach you some mighty valuable lessons. You might even end up lookin' like a lady...'

8

The Cure For Defiance

The sun was climbing into the sky when they rode out of town. It was early, with only a few people up and about, a good thing because he didn't want the girl to be seen. For one thing, her hands were tied before her with the red-checked cotton cloth. Also, her face bore scratches from the fight the previous night. A lawman like Phil Peake might have asked questions – but he wasn't around. And the girl's father wasn't in sight; maybe fatigue had overtaken him or maybe he'd gone for a horse. Matt had smuggled the girl out of the hotel by a back door. He took the gag from her mouth after they left the livery with two horses, one his mount from the T-Bar-T.

She spat cotton threads and epithets at him from the start. 'You – you big, hell-bent swine! You–'

'Get rid of them swear words,' he advised. 'Where you're goin', ladies like civilized speech. You won't like 'em at first. But they were used to the worst she-cats in Texas so you won't worry them none…'

He wouldn't explain further. He seemed to derive amusement from his secret thoughts. The horses, rested, well-fed and watered, moved briskly, soon putting Three Forks well behind them. There was no chance that Liza Backus might escape; he had a lead rope from his saddle pommel to the other animal, and he had his guns. She had nothing, no food or water, just the incredibly dirty clothes she stood in.

Matt Shayne had got to know the Marple sisters almost from the first week he had taken over the T-Bar-T. They were nesters on his land, at the far end of the rock-strewn valley. He had gone to look over the terrain and found the homestead. He had consulted his maps and deeds and sure enough Jane and Sarah Marple were living on his land. They had been in possession for about two years, using water from a good spring and keeping chickens, two Collie dogs and a cat. They also had a big potato and cabbage patch. A milking cow found enough grass to make her keep worthwhile. All the same, Matt had been puzzled as to how the two sisters could manage to live all the year on the meagre returns from the land. But then he got to talking and learned that they were straight, hard-working, God-fearing, and they received small pensions from the notorious Lazaro State Prison in Texas. They had been women warders and had retired at an early age.

He had come to an arrangement about the homestead. He wanted to use the water for his herd, but the sisters could stay if they kept the spring clean and free from stones and weed. Later Matt had had many a good meal and a chat with Jane and Sarah Marple.

During the ride there was time to reflect about Jimmy Skinner. He knew he couldn't ditch the boy. He'd have to see Judge Burch. He'd have to earn Jimmy's confidence and find out the truth about his trip to Three Forks. In the meantime, Liza Backus would have the steam taken right out of her.

The yellow, sandy canyon led straight to the homestead, an unexpected sight to a rider rounding the white, sun-bleached walls of rock. It was still morning when they dropped thankfully from the saddles. Matt Shayne was hungry. He knew he'd be made welcome at the table of Jane and Sarah Marple but, of course, there'd be some explaining to do.

'I've got a visitor for you,' he called out. 'This is Liza Backus.'

Jane Marple replied first. 'I'm Jane. How do you do?' Her clear grey eyes flicked over the dirty clothes without surprise. And then came Sarah's equally cool greeting:

'Pleased to meet you, my dear.' Again calm eyes smiled and awaited further explanations.

136

Matt chuckled and said, 'Liza would like to stay with you – maybe a week or two – just so she can learn some manners.'

'Manners? Surely you must be joking, Matt Shayne.' Sarah Marple, older than her sister by two years, smiled back. She stood tall and lean. Like Jane, she wore a long calico dress with a high waist. Both women kept their hair in coiled buns at the back of the neck. In fact, they were very much alike. They smiled at Matt and the glowering girl from the veranda of their spacious shack.

'Do come in, Matt,' Sarah said. 'Set yourself down and have coffee and something to eat. I know you like apple pie and steak.'

'I ain't goin' inside that lousy shack!' Liza cried. Then she spat at Matt. 'You just get these ties offen my wrists. First chance I get, I'll claw them damned eyes outa your sockets.' She jigged her horse close to him and tried to push the animal against him. When he just smiled at this move, she kicked at his shins. He avoided that by inches. She then tried to beat at his face with her bound fists. He had to hold her with one hand, leaning in the saddle.

'See what I mean, Jane and Sarah?' he called out. 'Liza is a bundle of fury. She doesn't like me. I reckon she won't like you two ladies either.'

'Oh, dear, that will be a pity.' Sarah Marple came forward. 'But I've always found that hatred disappears in the face of kindness – and we are always kind, aren't we, Jane?'

'Always – and with the worst that the devil could breed.' Jane sighed. 'My goodness, at Lazaro we had some terrors – women who had killed and robbed and who would do it again after they were released. But, Matt, I think you ought to explain further about Liza.' Jane Marple stared quizzically. 'She's really a pretty girl. Now, if she got rid of those terrible clothes…'

With anger crinkling her face, Liza Backus tried to free herself from Matt's grip. But Sarah Marple held her arm. Liza was surprised at the strength in the woman's fingers. There was fine authority in the grip. But this did not make Liza Backus kindly disposed towards the woman. She glared her defiance.

'You two can't keep me here! I'll just run like hell! You two old coyotes mean nothin' to me. I ain't takin' any notice of you.'

Sarah Marple looked critically at the dirty, frayed black shirt and the ill-fitting black pants that must have been made for a man. She shook her head as she looked at the girl's stringy black hair. She raised Liza's hand and looked disapprovingly at the grime under the fingernails. Then she gave a glance at the scuffed riding boots that would have disgraced a range bum.

'Terrible,' she muttered. 'But clothes can change a personality. Don't you know that? A nice dress can make a woman feel good – even frivolous. And mannish clothes are just awful.'

'You're loco!' said Liza Backus. 'I ain't taken up with clothes.'

'You should like nice things.'

'I'll tear 'em to shreds if you figure you can doll me up!'

'Really? Not after you've had a bath…'

'Water? I ain't gettin' into no cold water!'

'Warm water, dear – in a huge wood tub with lots of nice-smelling soap…'

'I'll get me back into my old duds – just you see,' yelled the girl.

'But they'll be burned.'

'I won't change! I'm a Backus – and I want to tell you two women somethin'. I'll kill this lousy gunny some day. He shot down my two brothers!'

'Oh dear, it seems you've got a lot of explaining to do, Matt Shayne.' Sarah Marple began to steer the girl to the house. 'You can tell me everything over a meal – and Liza will come to the table washed and in a clean dress.'

The operation took an hour, and by that time Matt Shayne was really hungry. He told Jane Marple about the Backus family, the way her brothers had died and how the girl had tried to kill him. 'She really hates me…

I'm not blaming her for that ... but I want her out of my hair. Now, if you and Sarah can tame her, show her some womanly manners ... just change her... I'll be grateful. And then maybe I'll get back to ranching...'

The door opened and Matt stared in amazement as a new person walked into the living room. A girl, slim in a waist-hugging cotton frock that was just her size, her dark hair freshly brushed into a sheen and coiled at the nape of her neck, eyes gleaming. She stood in shining black leather shoes, the toes peeping from under the dress. The sug-gestion of lithe limbs showed through the simple frock. Her bare arms were clean and utterly feminine.

But her tongue lashed out just the same. 'All right, so you've dolled me up – but I ain't changed.' She pointed a finger at Matt. 'I hate you. I'll kill you – just you see. And then I'll get me back to my pa.'

'Let's have our meal,' said Sarah Marple soothingly. 'My goodness, you both must be starving.'

'Good food takes the anger out of most people,' observed Jane.

Liza Backus sat down at the table, her arms folded, her eyes sparking her challenge at Matt Shayne. Strangely, he felt uncomfortable, and his gaze was drawn repeatedly to her soft neck and the swell of her breasts under the bodice of the dress.

Some time later he made his farewells and took the two horses from the small corral. Mounted, he looked back at the three women on the veranda. 'I'll be back, maybe in about a week. Teach Liza that she's a woman and that there's something better for her than hating and living like an animal in the hills.'

He rode out. There were many things on his mind. Apart from the work he was neglecting on his spread, he had to see Judge Burch about Jimmy Skinner. If he got the threat of the home for waifs and strays removed from the boy, he would be happier. Judge Burch was a considerate man who would listen to reason, but he would want the truth about the burning of Roper Stell's factory shed.

Matt Shayne had to skirt the trail that led down to the valley and the T-Bar-T. He was tempted to go back home, see his two hands and get some work done, even if it was only for a few hours. He halted the horses near a big red rocky outcrop and pondered. Then he shook his head. He couldn't turn his back on the boy. Something about the kid nagged at him; maybe he'd have been the same if he'd had as few chances as Jimmy Skinner. As it was, his own life wasn't exactly perfect. He had taken to the gun and killed men. It had always been in self-defence or in pursuit of the lawless, but he had become a killer. He wasn't proud of it, and if people would only leave him alone, he'd hang up his guns.

He kneed the horse back to the other trail, picking a slow way through grass clumps and cactus. Heat was flaring back from the dry land, and his horse's hoofs raised dust that somehow found its way into his mouth.

He stopped again after a mile to drink water from his canteen and dribble some onto his hand for the horses to lick.

The slow ride took him back to the green lands and the clumps of timber, then he headed for Three Forks.

He was passing the stockyards when a man nudged a dispirited black horse out of an alley and blocked his path.

'Hey! Where the hell's Liza? What've you done with her? I've been snoopin' all around town for a sign of her...'

It was Bill Backus, huddled in a black coat much too big for him. His nondescript hat was rammed on his untidy hair, concealing his bald spot. His gun was hidden somewhere under the voluminous coat and one thing was certain – a quick draw would be impossible.

'Liza? Well, now, I don't rightly know.' Matt Shayne regarded the other with disinterest. 'After she tried to kill me last night, she moseyed out. I put her out of my room...'

'You're a goddamn liar!'

Matt nodded. 'Maybe ... but don't make a habit of calling me names.'

'You seem all-fired pleased about something...'

Matt turned his horse around the other's mount and went down the main stem, presenting a broad back to Bill Backus. The man thrust a red, wet lower lip out in an ugly leer, then he felt for the shooting iron under his coat. But there were people on the boardwalks. A man was painting a sign and staring down from his ladder. A rancher leaned against his wagon, smoking a pipe.

Matt called at the sheriff's office and was allowed to see Jimmy Skinner. The deputy had let him in; it seemed that Phil Peake was out on business. And, the deputy told him, Judge Burch was due to roll in on the afternoon stage from Lamesa.

Jimmy Skinner was coiled on the cell bunk. He stared back at Matt with a set face. 'Howdy; Jimmy.'

'Get me out of here.'

'I'm trying, boy. I'll see Judge Burch pretty soon.'

'But he's on the side of the law. You could bust me out of here. Just put a gun in that deputy's back…'

'That would just make everything worse, Jimmy – you should know that.'

'My pa would have done it.'

'I doubt it. Even your father would know when the odds were stacked against him. Now look, Jimmy, what's the truth about your visit to town the other night? Did you set fire to Roper Stell's place?'

'No!'

Matt nodded. 'Good. I believe you…'

'Why should you? I could be lying. I could fool you.'

'You'd just let yourself down…'

'What d'you mean?'

'You won't be able to look me in the eyes, Jimmy, if you're lying – and that's a lousy feeling.'

The boy sighed. 'Honest, I went to town that night with the gun, figuring to kill that little snake for what he done to my pa. But then I changed my mind. I rode back and took a pot-shot at somethin' on the trail – might have been a coyote.'

Matt nodded. 'You were going to tell me all that the other day, but then you got defiant. All right, I understand.' Matt rubbed his chin. 'Well, I think it all depends on the judge. Would you like to come back to the T-Bar-T? Judge Burch might want to see you and hear your story – in fact, I'm sure of it.'

'Gosh, Mr Shayne, I don't want to go to no home.'

Matt went out on that. Nodding to the deputy, he walked to the street and his horse at the tie-rail. He decided to use the facilities offered by Violet Denton and get cleaned up. He wanted to make a good impression on Judge Burch.

As he led his horse thoughtfully along the busy road he didn't see Bill Backus in the shade of a falsefront. The man's bearded face was a mask of hatred.

Violet Denton seemed pleased to see Matt, but he was no better than most men at seeing into a woman's mind, so he didn't know she was angry with him.

She had been to his bedroom and had seen the torn drapes, a chair with a broken leg, all the signs of a fight. He had disappeared early that morning without as much as a word. But she had made enquiries because her feminine curiosity was aroused. And after she had spoken to the liveryman at the back of the hotel, she was really incensed.

'I reckon it was a girl,' the hostler had told her. 'Waal, she was dressed in a rannigan's clothes – mighty dirty at that – but I figure it was a gal. They rode out, figuring I wasn't around, but I was just standin' quiet in a corner.'

Violet had gone back to the bedroom for another look around. The chair with shreds of cotton cloth still around it puzzled her. The displaced water jug didn't add up. And then she noticed the slit pillow.

'A fight – with a girl.' Then she had it.

'That damned Backus bitch. What happened? God, did she stay all night in the room? He turns me down – and fools around with that unspeakable bitch. Hell, he must have forced himself on her because she hates his guts.'

Although her mind rushed on vindictively, she couldn't see how it had all happened. Some parts of it didn't make sense. Then, bitterly, thinking that Matt Shayne had preferred the wild, unwashed girl to herself, she trembled with fury.

So, when he called at The Splendide, seeking a drink and a wash-up, she smiled charmingly but seethed inwardly. 'Why, hello, Matt. A drink? Of course – any time.'

'I've got to see Judge Burch later. He doesn't expect me, but I want to see him about the Skinner boy.'

'Are you still concerning yourself with that brat?'

'Violet, he's a good kid. I know that Caleb Dray and Stell want him sent packin' to a home for waifs and strays.'

'Well, won't that do him good?'

He regarded her steadily: 'You know these homes are damned hard places.'

'Good enough for a brat like that Skinner boy.'

He narrowed his eyes. He wasn't entirely naïve about women and there was something in Violet's manner that wasn't right. Of course, she had no sympathy for Jimmy Skinner. But there was something else. Maybe she was just touchy today.

He reached for her arm and she jerked away. 'Don't paw, Matt. A drink, you said? Sure, why not?'

'I'll get me a good clean-up first and join you,' he said. 'I think I've got an hour before Judge Burch arrives.'

He entered the comfortable lounge a bit later, looking spruce for a range rider. He sank into a deep leather chair and not for the first time he looked appreciatively at the rich, red wallpaper and the gleaming mahogany woodwork. A bottle of Colonel Sanders' whiskey and a glass was on the table.

'Aren't you goin' to join me?' he asked.

'I don't feel like the stuff today,' she said.
'Well, I'm not a hard drinker, but here goes...'

She watched him pour a generous measure and drink part of it. Their eyes met and she smiled.

She was adept at forming words. 'So nice of you to look me up, Matt. As I've said before, you look good in this establishment.'

'I'm really a toughened rangehand. I've got the smell of horses and cattle around me. Are you tryin' to seduce me, Violet?' He grinned.

For a second her eyes narrowed as the significance of the word 'seduce' hit her and she had a fleeting mental glimpse of a wild, dark-haired girl who smelled of animals and dirt. And this girl was close to Matt Shayne, being fondled by him, although protesting.

'What does it take to seduce you, Matt?' she asked.

She thought it was a dangerous question, but he held his smile. The verbal barb seemed to have no effect.

'This whiskey is good,' he returned. 'And the seat is too darned comfortable. It sure reminds me that the bronc I fork is as hard as iron.'

'Enjoy the drink, Matt.' She watched as he poured another measure.

'Sure you won't have one?'

'No, but you go ahead.' She even filled his glass again after he had taken only a sip. She had the feeling she ought to keep talking. 'You're a fool about that boy, Matt. What's he to you? Nothing. He'll do you no good except put folks against you. I think you should forget him. Keep out of it. Why, his father was dirt.'

If she was trying to rile him, her whiskey was having an ameliorating effect and he just smiled. He drank deeply of the Colonel Sanders and grinned fuzzily at her. Moments later he began to yawn. He blinked his eyes and tried to rise, but Violet Denton pushed him down.

'You're not going anywhere, Matt Shayne,'

she whispered. 'You won't see Judge Burch. You'll be asleep. That boy can just get the hell out of your life – fast, I hope.'

Matt Shayne fought the drowsiness, tried to keep open eyelids that felt like little sheets of lead. But the whiskey had been neatly laced and he fell back, eyes shut, out to the world.

'You should know I keep a nice line in knockout drops, Matt Shayne,' murmured Violet. 'In a place like this, they sometimes come in handy.'

She contemplated him for a long time. Then she went for her handyman, a big black man who would take Matt to a room upstairs and keep his mouth shut.

Maybe they'd take Jimmy Skinner away that afternoon. He would be consigned to a home long before Matt could make a move.

And she would find out something about that wretched Backus girl. She would get to know what had happened. The girl had to be around somewhere.

Violet Denton had no idea that the girl's

father was watching the hotel from across the road and scheming to get even with Matt Shayne.

9

The Snatched Boy

The conference that late afternoon in the sheriff's office was short, vehement and decisive. Two men did most of the denouncing: Caleb Dray, who smoked a large cigar after carefully draping his coat over the back of a chair; and Roper Stell, who perched like a vindictive dwarf on a wooden stool, his fists clenched and his lower lip trembling with annoyance.

'He ruined me!' Stell piped. 'My shed – burned to the ground. I tell you, Judge Burch, we would be failing in our duty to the community if we let this young thug free. We–'

'You ain't ruined, Stell,' Sheriff Phil Peake put in. 'If you lost a dollar bill, you'd squeal like a hog goin' to the slaughterhouse. But I agree, the boy is a problem.'

'He has threatened my life and my property,' said Caleb Dray swiftly. 'Frankly, I see no alternative but to send him to a home. There's a suitable place at Lamesa.'

'Little better than a convict settlement,' muttered Phil Peake.

'What did you say, Sheriff?' Judge Burch sent his enquiring grey-eyed gaze at the lawman. He was a dignified man, as befitted his occupation, leaning towards portliness, and he'd had considerable experience of dealing with hardcases and the temporarily unfortunate. Sympathy was something he had learned to ration sparingly.

'That home is kind of hard,' Peake said. 'A newspaper editor in Lamesa called it a hell-hole. But I ain't seen the place...'

'Then you can hardly pass an opinion,' said the judge. 'I know something about the home, Sheriff. It's well-staffed and it places a terrible burden on the town finances. They have to make the boys work. Money does not grow on trees.'

'I figured Matt Shayne was interested in the boy,' grunted the sheriff. 'But he's not here – and he must know we're discussing the youngster. My deputy says he called here earlier.'

'That damned gunman is actively encouraging lawlessness in this lad!' shrilled Roper Stell. 'A gunhand! Totally unsuitable. God, he'll teach the boy to shoot! I tell you, that boy will try to kill us all one day.'

Caleb Dray nodded. 'I agree with that. Send him to the home in Lamesa. I don't know why we're wasting time on this subject. I personally, have business to attend to.'

The sheriff turned to the window. 'Maybe I should go look for Shayne. I think he wants to stand bond for the boy.'

'Doesn't he know I'm back in town?' asked Judge Burch.

'He should, sir. I guess he should...'

'Then if he can't bother to turn up, we will not consider him,' said the judge coldly.

'The boy, Jimmy Skinner, goes to the Lamesa home. See to it, Sheriff, first thing tomorrow. I'll sign the papers tonight and you can dispatch him on the morning stage with an escort. Heaven help us! The cost of justice is increasing every week. Now we have to keep the sons of scoundrels. Ah, well!' The judge consulted his gold watch. 'I'm tired. Good evening, gentlemen.'

That night, with Matt Shayne in a state of drugged unconsciousness that was to last almost round the clock, Bill Backus was active in the saloons. He listened to gossip, and even bought a drink for an old-timer who knew Peake's deputy. He got to know about the meeting in the sheriff's office, and he heard about the boy, Jimmy Skinner.

'Sending him to that home in Lamesa,' said the toothless old man. 'Why, I knowed Mick Skinner – the gosh-darned sneak-thief! I knowed who stole them hogs outa the pens that night – it was Mick Skinner. They was hog-meat the next morning. I remember he tried to sell me a horse one

158

day, but I saw the blotted brand, yes, sir, I did.'

'This boy – I hear he set fire to Stell's place,' Backus said.

'Sure – everyone knows that.'

'I heard that Matt Shayne, the new owner of the T-Bar-T, wanted to keep that young squirt and bring him up. Is that so?'

'Waal, I did hear that, mister.' The old man laughed drunkenly. 'I hear about everythin' in this town. You know somethin' – the deputy is my son-in-law. Yup!' He nodded. 'Sure, I'll take another drink. Yes, sir, that Shayne feller wanted to bring that boy up. Crossed Stell and Dray on account of it. I figure that boy won't be long in Lamesa. Shayne will go get him outa there. Say, d'you know that Shayne feller is a top gunhand?'

'He's a snake!' said Bill Backus, unable to take that kind of admiration any longer.

He went into the night air and spat in the roadway. 'I ain't done with Mr Shayne – not by a long chalk, by hell!'

Jimmy Skinner was placed on the stage at exactly nine o'clock the next morning, escorted by a deputy. Sheriff Phil Peake watched grimly, dissatisfied. He had loathed Mick Skinner as a lawman, and he had reservations about the boy, but Phil Peake had been brought up as a member of a large family and he had strong opinions about the value of family life. If Matt Shayne had come forward to take charge of the boy, in spite of his former reputation as a gunny, he'd have backed his claim.

But Matt Shayne did not appear. No one seemed to know his whereabouts.

'Backed out, by heaven,' grunted the sheriff. 'Waal, it figures. That boy ain't nothing to him.'

The stage drew out a few minutes late with its six passengers. Jimmy stared stonily ahead. He felt sure that Matt Shayne had abandoned him. In spite of all the fine talk, the promises, he wasn't wanted. Mr Shayne hadn't even turned up. He'd heard that

160

from the sheriff. Mr Shayne had not even seen the judge. So it was all talk! Well, one thing was sure – Lamesa wouldn't hold him long. He'd get out. Maybe he'd come back to Three Forks and kill the skunks who'd hanged his father. He'd do it. He had years in which to plan revenge.

The man who followed the stage for the first ten miles was hard put to match the speed of the four-horse team because his black horse was in a poor condition. Bill Backus rowelled and cursed the reluctant beast as the stage became nothing more than a cloud of dust far ahead on the winding trail. He began to catch up when the stage halted at the relay depot. He approached warily, his horse blown, his thoughts chaotic and only the haziest of plans in his mind. He could think of only one point; the boy was a key to revenge. Shayne had given the youth food, shelter and support. Why he had allowed him to be taken to Lamesa was a bit of a mystery. Maybe Shayne figured to turn up at the Lamesa home for waifs and strays and claim the boy. That had to be Shayne's idea. Seemed the louse had lingered too long with the curvy owner of The Splendide – well, that was too bad.

Shayne had killed his two sons. Now if he could set hands on that young squirt, he could make Shayne suffer. He was pretty sure that Matt Shayne had welcomed the boy to his home, had been like a father to him. Well, Shayne would find out what it was like to see kith and kin suffer, bleed and finally die. All he had to do was snatch that boy.

Now, if Liza was with him, she could have helped. What in tarnation had happened to her? He had last seen her climbing up to give Shayne his come-uppance. He had waited until exhausted. Had Liza got frightened? Something had happened. He hardly knew what to think. Well, he'd find the girl again. She'd turn up. Maybe that smart-alec galoot had scared her off. One sure thing – she hadn't succeeded in killing him. He was riding around as large as life.

Bill Backus stared sourly at the motionless stage. The driver and passengers had apparently gone into the depot for refreshments. The horses had been changed for the haul into Lamesa. They would not stop long at the depot. Now where was the lad? Had he any chance of snatching him? Or was the idea crazy?

He hitched the black horse to a nearby rail and strode into the yard. Then a blur of movement inside the stage caused him to stare hard. He saw a face for a moment.

Hardly crediting his luck, Bill Backus moved swiftly to the stage. He glanced through a window and saw the boy. He grinned as he noted the lad was tied by his wrists and one end of the rope was looped around a door handle.

'So they figured to leave you out here,' said the old man. He whipped out a knife from a belt under his shapeless coat. 'Waal, that sure beats all! Backus, you sure get mighty good hunches! I figured there'd be a break.'

163

He climbed into the stage, then he cut through the rope binding Jimmy's wrists and began dragging the boy out of the stage.

'C'mon – we got to hurry!'

'You're Bill Backus! I don't want to go with you!'

'You know me, huh? Now look, squirt, I'm takin' chances to set you free. You want to be free? You don't want to see the inside of that home in Lamesa, do you?'

'No. But I don't want to go with you. Get out of my way, mister – I'm gonna run for it.'

'Not so fast.' Bill Backus grabbed Jimmy's vest, a flapping over-large garment that Phil Peake had provided. 'You're goin' with me. I got a horse – you wouldn't get far on foot, young feller.'

'I don't know why you're doin' this,' Jimmy said. 'I know you. You tried to gun down Matt Shayne and then you fought him. But he beat you.'

'Yeah – you and the whole town knows that.' Bill Backus dragged the boy over the dusty yard, looking back at the depot building, fearful that any moment might bring discovery.

Bill Backus suddenly hauled out his gun and pushed it cruelly against the boy's side. 'Now get movin'. You figure to risk a slug?'

'You wouldn't shoot!' Jimmy yelled. 'The noise would bring 'em all out – the deputy and the driver. You'd end up in the hoosegow, mister.'

Because the seconds were flying by and time was vital, Bill Backus cursed the youngster's obstinacy. Jimmy's wits were quick. He began to struggle. He was so lithe he'd be free in a matter of minutes if something wasn't done.

The Backus man did the only thing that came naturally to him. As the boy fought in his grip, he brought the gun barrel down firmly on the side of the lad's head. Jimmy Skinner sagged. The man held him; then he carried him back to where the patient horse stood with head down and ears pricked to catch any strange sounds.

Grunting and cursing, Bill Backus lifted the unconscious boy across the saddle and then, foot in stirrup, he urged the black horse away from the stage depot. He flung a few backward glances, scarcely believing his good luck. It seemed the passengers and crew of the stage were still enjoying their break. A gust of male laughter came to his ears. Yeah, somebody had told a joke. Well, that was fine. Maybe he had time to get clear away.

He knew he would be lucky to travel far before the stage was ready to roll out on the remainder of the trip to Lamesa. But if he could find some place to hole up and evade a search, that would be fine. Then he could figure out the rest of his plan.

Heeling at the animal, Backus sent it flying across the flats, heading for a shale hollow. He followed the depression until it widened into a small canyon. He was glad when he saw the canyon floor was mostly loose shale because that would leave a trail it would take an Apache to track. He urged his mount on.

When he saw the numerous cave mouths on the side of the yellow canyon wall, he was sure that this was the answer. He would hole up with the boy. He could hide the horse. Pursuers would have the whole wide territory to search. They might not even come this way. And they might figure that the boy had got a knife and cut himself free.

Without wasting time on doubts, he headed his protesting horse up a dangerously narrow track that led up the canyon wall. The animal's hoofs slipped frequently, sending bits of shale sliding down to the canyon bed. Bill Backus cursed again, thinking the noise could be heard for miles. But that was just his nerves jabbing at him. He was, he estimated, a good mile from the stage depot. Sure, he had pulled a neat trick. The main idea still held good; he had the boy and could stab at Matt Shayne through that. He could give the man with the rep real hell, if he played his cards right – and maybe he'd end up gunning Shayne into the ground.

He had to dismount and lead his horse because the track became merely a ledge and there was real danger that if the animal slipped they could hit the ground with a thud. Then he saw signs that the boy was recovering his senses when a small, moaning sound escaped his lips.

Bill Backus dragged the horse into the first cave that was large enough to afford concealment. He held the leathers and led the animal back into the cave to a point where the daylight began to cut off. The hole was pretty big, littered with boulders, and it curved into the canyon wall.

Jimmy Skinner opened his eyes. He was lying on the cave floor. Bill Backus bent over him, chuckling. He had a length of rope ready.

'You hit me!' cried Jimmy. 'God, how my head aches!'

'Just shuddup and you'll be fine,' sneered Backus.

'You must be out of your mind, mister. What's the idea of all this?'

Bill Backus leered at him, the possibility of revenge now a certainty. 'That Shayne *hombre* will do anythin' to help you, boy. That's all I need to know. I can lure him out here and shoot him down, or I can send him one of your ears. I'll give him hell for what he done to my two sons. Now that's all you need to know.'

He began wrapping the old lariat around the boy's wrists. Jimmy struggled and earned a cuff on the side of the head. Eventually he was roped, hand and foot. Then Bill Backus shuffled to the cave mouth and stared into the bright, glaring canyon, hoping there would be no sign of pursuit. The whole arid land lay silent. He could see a long way and if anything moved out there he would spot it. The age-old canyon walls just brooded. He returned, chuckling, his brain conjuring up a plan.

'I'll get that Shayne *hombre* now!' He laughed. 'You'll bring him right into my gunsights, boy – after he gets one of your ears and sweats it out.'

'You're wrong, for a start,' said Jimmy scornfully.

'What do you mean by that, boy?'

'Matt Shayne don't want to have anythin' to do with me.'

'Why, sure he does! He was gonna raise you, warn't he?'

'Maybe – at one time. But I guess he changed his mind…'

'No.' Bill Backus pointed a finger ingrained with dirt. 'He saved you from a hangin', from what I was told. And he got you outa that Stell feller's hands. He was all set to help you.'

'He didn't turn up at the meeting with Judge Burch.'

Backus shrugged. 'So he got himself tied up with a female – somethin' a boy wouldn't understand. I tell you, he'll bust a gut to rescue you. I'm bankin' on that. And that's how I'll get him. Now I got to think. Maybe I should hole up here until night … maybe travel by the moon… I could take you to our shack up in the hills. Sure, that might be a good idea...'

'I think you're loco,' said Jimmy. 'I tell you, Matt Shayne don't want anythin' to do with me. He thinks I fired Stell's place.'

'Yeah, you did.'

'I didn't. It must've been an accident – or one of the other boys put a torch to it. They were always threatening to do that, but I didn't pay much attention.'

Bill Backus snarled back at him. 'Shuddup! I ain't interested. I figure he'll come hellin' after you. All I got to do is arrange it.'

The waiting period was long. Backus watched the sun go down and then the shadows on the canyon floor lengthened. He didn't dare venture out in daylight. It was a good bet the deputy would report back to the sheriff in Three Forks after his first fruitless search, and after that anything could happen. A posse could be out. Matt Shayne would hear about the missing youth. But it would be a mystery as to how he had got away.

They had to eat, and that helped pass the time. He had a saddle-bag full of scraps such as cooked sidemeat and some hard-tack biscuits. He leered at the boy and gave him a chunk of biscuit.

'Here – keep your gut filled.'

'I want a drink.'

'Ain't enough water. The horse comes afore you.'

When the sun dropped over the ridge of hills there was silvery moonlight. He felt safe.

'We're lightin' out, young feller. You'll sit the saddle in front of me with your hands tied – and if you try any tricks I'll gunbutt you again. You want another crack on the side of the head?'

Jimmy shrank from this violent man. It was far better to play it safe than take risks. But somewhere along the line he might get a chance to escape from this evil, dirty specimen of humanity.

But Bill Backus had the cunning of the animals he had hunted, and as they rode through the night he kept a careful eye on Jimmy, from time to time punching him hard in the ribs as a reminder that tricks would not pay. In this way, with the boy fearful and weary, they headed for the hills. He kept off the trails and saw no other riders. Eventually they were away from the cattle ranges, a silent man and a frightened boy on a tired horse.

The Backus family owned two shacks; one at the base of the hills and the other high among the timbered slopes where beaver could be found in the river. There were deer and elk in the forests, and there were fish. He and Red and Walt had lived good, caring for no man. If it was rough, that had been their affair. Liza had grown up in this mould. They had been a hard family, ready to argue and fight. Maybe he had forgotten that Liza was a girl – but that never worried her. Then Red had got into the fight with that lousy gunny while in town for a spell and now he was dead. Walt, too.

'Waal, I'll get even with him – just see!'

gritted Bill Backus as he rode on.

In the early hours of the morning they finally reached the first shack. Jimmy Skinner dropped to the ground while Bill Backus sullenly saw to the horse's comfort, taking the saddle off, pushing the weary beast into a stall and flinging some feed onto the ground.

Then the man and the boy went into the shack and prepared for sleep. Jimmy was tied to a bunk and some dry bread was thrown at him. Bill Backus made coffee, drinking greedily, then he fried bacon and bread and wolfed it down. Finally he curled up among blankets that stank to high heaven and soon he was asleep, snoring like a hog.

After some hours it was daylight, and the sound of birds chattering in the nearby trees awakened Backus.

He came close to the white-faced boy, a knife in his hand. 'I'm gonna lop off an ear. I need somethin' to send to that Shayne feller. I'm leavin' you here, then I'm ridin' for Three Forks, with your ear.'

10

The Wonder Of The New Liza

After the deputy got back to town with the news that the boy had escaped from the stage, Matt Shayne spent a restless night. A posse had gone out and returned, late at night, with no news of the missing Jimmy Skinner.

There was nothing he could do that night, unless he proposed to wander the trails blindly. He went to sleep after staring at the moonlit night from a hotel window. He had cleared out of The Splendide when he had awakened. His thick, yellowish tongue told him the story – and he had a headache to boot.

'You should buy a better brand of knockout drops, Violet,' he had told her grimly. 'It sure spoiled that whiskey.'

After the restless night he saddled a fresh horse; checked his guns, snicked the rifle snugly into the saddle holster and filled his water bottle. He had a bedroll and a grub bag. He was riding out, seeking sign – anything that would give him a lead to the missing boy.

He headed for the stage relay station as a start. He could talk to the depot man, get his version of what had happened.

But the man was tired of talking about the incident and he pointed out that he had work to do. 'That boy was sittin' in the stage – tied with rope to a door handle. I saw him myself. Don't ask me how come he got a knife. But I heard about that boy. Seems his old man got himself hanged – so maybe he was full of tricks.'

'A knife?' mused Matt Shayne. 'It isn't possible. He would be searched when he left the jail. How could he have a knife?'

'How in tarnation d'you expect me to answer that? The rope was sliced, mister, that's all I know.'

Matt stared over the land. A heat haze danced on a distant ridge. Turning to the disgruntled depot man, he said, 'The deputy escorting the boy must have ridden around looking for sign...'

'He sure did, but I get a lot of riders call in here and that trail is thick with hoofmarks.'

'But the boy would be on foot.'

'Waal, in that case he could be real dead by now, what with the heat by day and the cold at night.' As if terminating the interview, the man stamped away.

Matt went out to study trail marks in all directions, but he was no Indian scout and the exercise only left him puzzled.

He knew he was deeply involved. The fate of Jimmy Skinner had to be resolved. It was true, the boy could be dead – or dying – somewhere out there on the desert.

He had to call a halt to his wandering. There was an endless vista of ridges and valleys which could go right on to the pine-clad hills. Searching for sign was getting him nowhere. Maybe he needed help.

With sudden determination he began to push his horse, heading for the distant area beyond the numerous ridges where the T-Bar-T lay. He would get Sam Harper and Manuel Reyna and have them ride out with him on a wider search. Three men might achieve something. The task would mean taking the men away from ranch work, but that couldn't be helped.

When he finally reached the ranch, he was in a grim mood. He cursed Violet Denton. Never would he forgive that lady for the trick she had pulled. And never again would he drink her whiskey!

Hard-faced and dusty, irritated by the chore of saddle-sitting, Matt's mood was made really savage when Sam Harper handed him a small package and a message. 'An old range tramp came in here about an hour ago on a mule high as a house. He had a message from Bill Backus.'

'Backus?'

Sam Harper shifted uncomfortably. 'Look,

boss, I ain't so good at talkin' – so I'll just repeat the message. This old mule man said Backus has the boy and for proof there's his ear in that box.'

Matt Shayne felt every sinew go iron-hard. 'I don't believe it…'

'Well, boss, I ain't opened that package, as you can see. There's more to the message and I better get it off my chest afore I forget it. If you want the other ear, said this mule rider, you got to locate the Backus cabin at the base of the hills and then you'll be told where to find the boy.'

'You let that messenger go?'

'I tried to get tough with him, but he had met Backus somewhere out in the canyons and all he knew about was this box and the message he had to repeat.'

Matt held the small paper-wrapped box grimly. Backus was the only answer. Obviously the man had freed the boy from the stage; that was the way Jimmy had escaped. So Backus planned revenge, still nursing hatred for his lost sons. Jimmy was just a means to an end.

'His base cabin?' muttered Matt Shayne. 'Another ear?'

'That was the message, boss.'

Matt stared disdainfully at the small package, unwilling to open it. Worry lines cracked the dust on his face. Then, slowly, he began to tear the paper from the box. Finally he prised up the lid of the box.

He stared at the object lying inside the grubby white box. He didn't touch the thing.

'What is it, boss?'

'It's a lousy trick … to give me hell … he's playing with me…'

Sam stared at the contents of the box. 'It ain't right. That's not a real ear…'

Matt Shayne nodded and flung the box to the ground. 'It's a slice from a sow's ear.'

Sam looked up swiftly. 'Then he ain't got the boy.'

'He has him. He's spinning his tricks out, Sam.'

'You want us to come along?'

'No. I'll handle Backus alone.'

As he saddled a new mount, Sam Harper gave some information. 'You can locate that Backus cabin pretty easy. I was once up that way with another rider afore I worked for you, Mr Shayne, and he pointed out that Backus place. It's a climbing trail, plenty of timber and if you head for Spiral Peak you can't go far wrong.'

Matt nodded. He had seen Spiral Peak previously, as Sam knew, but from many miles distant. 'I'll get there.'

'Watch for tricks.'

'There are always tricks with that polecat.'

As he rode out of the ranch yard, Matt reflected that Bill Backus was more animal than man. Then he thought of Liza Backus. His line of riding would take him close to the canyon where the Marple sisters had their home. He could stop and talk to them about Liza. His horse would need watering and a rest by then.

The swift lope of his fresh horse had crystallized his thoughts; he knew that Bill

Backus wanted him dead and that holding the boy was only a means to get him there. He was being lured to that cabin.

Even as he thundered the horse into the canyon where Sarah and Jane had their smallholding, he knew he didn't really have to make this stop. He had to admit it – for some crazy reason he wanted to see Liza Backus.

He didn't know why. She hated him. She was impossibly wild, a true daughter of her unspeakable father. She, too, wanted to kill him. Maybe the girl had had real affection for her dead brothers.

He doubted, too, that the Marple sisters would have any lasting effect on Liza. And he couldn't expect them to put up with her for months. In fact, the girl might have vanished by now.

But, when he rode up to the neat picket fence around the house and hitched his horse, he was greeted by one woman only. She stood on the veranda and watched him calmly, her dark hair neat, her face clean and surprisingly beautiful. Liza smiled and walked slowly, gracefully, her pretty cotton dress curving to a shapely waist and leg.

'You,' she said. 'To what do we owe the pleasure?'

'You said that real nice – if a bit too polite.' He paused. 'I was ridin' by.' He tilted his new Stetson. 'Where are Jane and Sarah?'

Liza waved a hand to the back of the house. 'In the field – workin'. You want them?'

'I'll see them before I go – sure.' He didn't intend to say a word about her father. 'How are you doin'?'

'I haven't escaped...'

'Do you like Jane and Sarah?'

She smiled, her eyes meeting his, a gleam in their dark depths. 'They're nice folks ... when a girl gets to know them. They told me some stories about that State prison – makes you think how easy it is to end up like that.'

He couldn't smile; there were too many nagging worries locked in his mind. 'Yeah, there's a slippery slope, Liza. We could all make a big mistake and end up in jail. But tell me, what have you been doin'?'

There was a flash of the old defiance. Then she smiled. 'I guess I could have run off – if I'd wanted to walk for miles. Then … well, Jane and Sarah were kinda nice to me, but real firm, just like I was a daughter – or a younger sister. They started me on readin' again – that's something I never done since the days when I had my ma. Me – readin'. That's sure somethin'. And I done some needlework. Been a long time since I did anythin' fancy. Always too busy poundin' skins to keep 'em soft. And then the sisters said I talked too rough and snapped back too much. They made a bet I couldn't talk like a lady. I said I could. And that's what I'm doin' now.' Her smile was very wide, revealing her white teeth. 'Do you think I'm doin' fine, Mr Shayne?' The question held a touch of mockery. 'Do you like the way I talk? Do you figure I could hold my own with the ladies in Three Forks? Do you?

After all, this was your idea.'

He didn't reply. She was sure she could taunt him. She walked slowly down the veranda, throwing him a cool glance, her dark eyebrows emphasizing the softness of her skin. She turned, almost like an actress moving along a stage, and returned to him. 'Well?'

'You've changed.'

'Have I? Are you sure? After only a few days?'

'You don't have to live like an animal in a cave,' he ground out. 'You could be ... really beautiful...'

He had never meant to say such a crazy thing. But, if he was shocked at his own thoughts, the girl was equally surprised. She stood rigid for a moment, every line in her body betraying her startled reaction.

The silence was finally broken by Liza. 'Beautiful?' She was mocking him again. 'Really, Mr Shayne? I remember that you called me a she-cat...'

'You set out to kill me,' he countered.

A flush crept into her cheeks. She had to be really bold to stare back at this tall, lean man. There was, she knew, no anger left in her, although she couldn't be sure how long this strange ability to speak reasonably with him would last. Yes, she had sought to kill him once, with a knife, and she'd been prepared to watch his life blood pump out. Would she ever feel like that again? She had no way of knowing. But she was aware of a need inside her, something that made her want to reach out and touch this man, as if in spite of everything, she wanted to reassure him. Why this need, this yearning, should exist in her heart she did not know. But it was there.

'You killed Red and Walt,' she said quietly.

'I did,' he said, 'and I wish to God I hadn't. The same goes for all the other men, if you really want to know. When I came to the T-Bar-T, I planned to give up the gun for good, but they wouldn't let me...'

'Jane and Sarah told me about killers they knew in the State prison, women who had killed husbands and lovers. They became haunted by fears in their later years and were never normal, never–' The girl broke off. 'I could have killed you. I'm glad I didn't.'

'Why? You had good cause – you've still got cause.' It was his turn to mock.

She stared down at the veranda boards. 'I don't want to kill you...' It was a muttered, jerky reply. In that moment she in no way resembled the old wild Liza.

Then she looked him full in the eyes. 'I'm talking like a fool. I don't know what I'm saying. I'd better go...'

She ran from him, holding the hem of her skirt high enough to clear her feet.

Matt Shayne rammed a fist into his palm, then he turned, as confused as she was.

He strode down to the field to see Jane and Sarah, but he managed only a few words with them, saying he had to go.

'Have you seen Liza?' Jane asked.

'Yes. I – I talked to her...'

'She's not wicked, you know.'

'I know that, Jane,' he grated. 'And thanks for everything you're doing.'

'Call again when you have more time.'

'I'll do that.'

He was back in the saddle and riding out when he realized that he had to deal with Liza's father, and after that happened the girl might hate him more than ever.

Would he ever be free of the curse of the gun?

11

The Final Trick

Matt Shayne rode hard until Spiral Peak was on the horizon, then he slackened the horse's gait to a lope. From now on he had to be as wary as any stalked animal. The sun had passed its highest point and was descending in deep reddish hues. Hungry, he put off the empty stomach feeling with strips of cold cooked bacon and dry buns that had been made with beer. He swilled the meal down with water, swaying in the saddle to the horse's gait, his hands free of the leathers.

The trail ascended, snaking past boulders and fringed with trees where twittering jays told of his approach. He put the curious steeple of rock behind him. The horse had to scramble for footholds.

Then he saw the shack as he went around a rock outcrop. He immediately halted his mount.

Was Jimmy Skinner in that cabin?

Matt Shayne found a rocky nook in which to tether his horse. Then, taking his rifle, he walked forward. Every sense was tuned to pick up the slightest warning sound or movement. If Bill Backus was hoping he would walk into a dry-gulch, he would have to reckon with incredibly fast reaction, for Matt Shayne had walked into ambushes before and lived.

He halted ten yards from the cabin. The cabin seemed to possess an unnatural silence – or was it just his imagination? Why should there be any sound from the cabin? Why should he sense any movement? But the message the muleman had delivered had said he'd be told where to find the boy when he located the cabin. Of course, the whole thing could be a trick. In fact, with Backus it was bound to be a trick.

He levelled the rifle holding it waist-high. For a long time he just stood there, taking in every sound. A large leaf from a nearby sycamore, floating to the ground because the stalk had withered, attracted his eye. He watched it settle.

He had to move. He was a perfect target. If Backus was waiting to ambush him, he wouldn't have a better chance than now. The man could be hidden. There were plenty of rocky clefts. If he intended a fast, accurate bullet to end his vendetta, why had he waited this long?

More urgent than a gun encounter was the need to discover Jimmy Skinner but maybe that would coincide with the killing slug. He would be of little use to the boy then.

He was tempted to walk on, straight to the cabin, in the hope that Bill Backus was a poor shot, or that he was waiting until the door was opened before triggering.

Matt's finger itched against the trigger guard of the rifle. He felt like blasting a round of shells at the cabin, as if that would destroy its menace. But that was wildness nudging into his mind. He rejected it. A round of shots might kill the boy he was trying to save.

The waiting game told him one thing – Backus wasn't waiting to pot-shot him like a bottle on a wall. It was something else.

Some other trick? His imagination seized on the notion, churning it many ways so that all possibilities should be examined. Some other way of killing him! What could the old mountain man cook up?

He knew he had to look inside the cabin to find out if Jimmy was there – or some grisly reminder of him. There was only one way now.

Matt leaped ahead, legs pistoning in long strides, his gun pointed and ready to shoot. He reached the cabin door, then rammed it back on its leather hinges as he dived inside.

He slid on the earth-packed floor, gun and eyes scanning the bare place. He saw the bunks, but no one was here. Thoughts raced through his brain, seeking an explanation.

There had to be one. The man with two dead sons wasn't playing games.

The mocking shout came from a long way off. It was Backus, unable to resist a final taunt. Unwittingly, he was giving himself away.

'You – Shayne – you're dead! I've got you!'

If the man had kept his mouth shut, he would have succeeded. A flash of intuition tore through Matt's brain and sent him lunging for the cabin door.

He had to get out!

He nearly tore the cabin door from its hinges as he crashed through. He ran like a man with the fear of hell on him. As he ran, he half expected to feel the tearing thump of destruction hit him in the back. Then would come total oblivion.

It came, but it was seconds too late. Bill Backus had paid for his error. His triumphant taunt had cost him victory. The explosion tore the cabin apart, sending timber hurtling into the air. A blast of air hit Matt Shayne square in the back. He was lifted off his feet by the blast and rammed to the earth. Stunned, he lay still. Rock debris, sods from the cabin roof and shattered timber fell all around him.

From a sheltered cranny Bill Backus had seen his victim run from the cabin. Cursing, he had dived for the explosive plunge. He had rammed it down, feeling sure he would still get the man he hated so much. The tearing roar of the explosion had forced him down. When he looked up, there was dust swirling all around the place where the cabin had stood.

He felt sure he had got Shayne. The blast must have got him. But how the man had guessed the shack was rigged with explosives was impossible to understand. Shayne had instincts that were not human. He was too quick. But the blast must have hit him. The exploding shack would have rammed into him. He hadn't got clear.

It had been a neat trick. They'd had the dynamite for some time, intending to blast a rock face that Walt had sworn contained gold. They had the wiring, the batteries and all the gear. Walt had known all about it, he'd even shown him how to set it up. What Walt hadn't guessed was that it would be used to avenge his own death.

Bill Backus stood up and surveyed the wreck of the base shack. The place didn't mean much to him. The cabin in the hills was more important.

He stared, wondering where he would find the body of the man who had killed Walt and Red. He wanted to see it, to gloat over the bloodied corpse. He'd kick it. He'd hack at it. He'd leave it as food for coyotes and buzzards. It was all the carcass was good for.

He came down from his perch intent on the gruesome search. An odd thought flickered through his brain; he had no need of the boy now. He could set off, on foot, and if he made it, well, that was his luck. No one would want to listen to his story, anyway.

Bill Backus trudged down the slope, his gaze searching for the sign of a body. With savage triumph, he saw it and laughed.

Matt Shayne lay in a hole, motionless, a length of torn timber across his legs. He was face-down and covered in dust.

Bill Backus leaned over the body; grabbed the shirt collar and began to roll it over. He saw Matt's bloodied face, then the man's eyes opened and stared at him challengingly. At the same time, a gun appeared in Matt's hand and was pointed at the older man's stomach.

'Where's the boy?' Matt demanded.

'Tied, just up the slope.'

'I hope for your sake that he's all right.' Matt sat up. He had been hit on the head with a flying stone. The timber across his legs had not broken anything but he'd received a nasty thump from it.

Matt got to his feet and moved close to the trapper. He took the gun from the holster under the shapeless coat. 'You won't want this.' He threw the weapon into the nearby rocks. 'Now, take me to the boy.'

Bill Backus stumbled ahead. At one point

he halted, his feet on mossy rocks, and glared. 'I could leave that boy tied up – you might not ever find him.'

'And I could kill you,' said Matt. 'Eventually I'd find the boy. Now – get.'

The boy was lying in a cleft between rocks, higher up the tree-clad slope from the spot where Backus had detonated his dynamite. The boy was tied and gagged.

'You all right, boy?' Matt asked as he removed the gag.

'I'm fine, Mr Shayne. Just hungry – and scared. I thought the dynamite had got you.'

As Matt Shayne attended to the boy, rubbing some feeling into his numb wrists, Bill Backus figured he could make a break for it. He had seen the gun holstered again as Matt gave the boy attention. He had a horse tethered not so far away among the trees...

He raced down the rock-strewn slope, at an impossible speed for a man his age. He couldn't control his downward plunge. Matt drew his gun and then hesitated. What good would it do to kill this old man? Let him go!

But the downhill run came to a disastrous end for the trapper. One moment he was plunging crazily through boulders and then he tripped and went head-first into a cleft. As he fell a cry tore from his throat, then there was silence.

When Matt Shayne bent over him minutes later he saw that the man was dead, his neck broken by the fall against the hard rock. There was nothing anyone could do for him.

Matt straightened, feeling the old weariness and distaste for death. He, the death dealer, was sick and tired of it all.

A flashing thought about Liza hit him. Here was another death for her to swallow, another story he had to explain; but at least he hadn't killed the man. It had been an accident. Jimmy Skinner could back that up.

'Come on, boy,' he muttered. 'Let's get to the horses. Backus must have one somewhere...'

Matt buried the old man, then they rode

away, down the hillside, in the direction of the T-Bar-T.

'That's where you'll be stayin', Jimmy boy, from now on.'

With the boy in the care of Sam Harper, he set off for Three Forks although it would be late at night before he reached the place. He wanted to report to the sheriff and settle the whole issue.

With the lamps burning yellow in his office, Phil Peake stared at the hard-ribbed rancher. 'You're tryin' to tell me old Backus is dead – and buried? You didn't shoot him?'

'You can dig him up if you want to,' said Matt Shayne.

'I might do that. And I'll sure talk to that boy...'

'Any time. Make it tomorrow. I want this cleared up.'

'All right, Mr Shayne, you've got yourself a deal,' Phil Peake lumbered to his feet, stroking his moustache. 'You goin' to Violet Denton's place tonight?'

'Not a chance.'

'Don't like the whiskey, huh?' Peake grinned. 'After what you've told me about it, I don't blame you. Waal, I've got news for you, Shayne. I don't like the hell you've kicked up around this town of mine, but there has to be an end to it and I accept that the Backus family leaned on you. So I'll support you in your claim for the boy. I figure you might be good for him. I take it he won't run away...'

'He's tired of runnin' – tired of being kicked around. He'll settle down and learn ranching. Maybe he's like me – I'm tired of the hell-around, too.'

'I've been askin' questions ... them boys Stell had workin' for him ... they fired the damned place. An age-old idea – revenge on the master...'

'Good. That's one accusation less against Jimmy.'

Phil Peake suddenly laughed. 'Imagine you tryin' to make a lady out of that she-cat! If that don't beat all. The crazy ideas you get, Shayne. Still, it's better than tryin' to kill the whole Backus lot.'

Matt walked into the night air. He went to a hotel, booked in, had a few drinks and a hot water wash before he finally slid gratefully between the sheets.

Next day he had one last duty; he had to ride out and tell Liza about her father.

There were delays. Judge Burch sent for him. When Matt finally rode out of Three Forks, he didn't realize that Peake had already sent a deputy out to tell the girl about her father's death.

After a swift ride he pulled the tired horse up at the tie rail outside the neat shack belonging to the Marple sisters. The animal snorted, shook its head with a jingle of the steel rings in its bridle, and then it pawed the earth.

For some reason Liza had expected him and she tore furiously onto the veranda boards. 'You killed him! You killed him – you liar!'

She was wearing the dirty clothes of the old Liza Backus. She ran to him, her hands outstretched to claw at his eyes. She blamed him, although the deputy had said that her father had met with an accident and was dead.

She had even dirtied her face and hands. Her hair hung down her neck, swishing wildly as she moved at him. As she struck, he held her hands. He had to control her.

'You're a killer! You lowdown skunk!' She used some filthy invective that she had learned from her family. Finally, breathless, she gasped, 'You wanted him dead – you ain't fit to live and I'm still gonna kill you. So you figured you could change me. Well, I'm the last of the Backus lot and I hate you. I won't change. You and your smart tricks can't make me.'

'Liza – believe me, it was an accident. He fell and broke his neck. I had to come over to tell you but it seems somebody got here before me. Liza, please calm down. There's no going back for you. You can't live in the hills.'

'I can! I will! You can go to hell. Let go of

me! I'll claw your eyes out. I'll–'

'Liza – change your clothes, then calm down and we'll talk. I've got to explain.'

She kicked at his shins. Her eyes were shining with a wild rage, an unnatural glint that no words could dispel. He just had to hold her and for this she screamed her fury at him.

Then Jane and Sarah came and took the girl away.

Matt Shayne returned to his horse. Dismayed, he was sure that Liza had reverted to her old wild, hating self. She was back to wanting him dead. He still had one more enemy and the thought sickened him.

He rode hard to get away from the scene, away from the knowledge that the girl hated him. He had the rotten feeling that he had solved nothing.

He stayed away for three days and then Jane Marple rode over to the T-Bar-T in a small gig.

'You've got to come and see her,' Jane said.

'She'll probably try to knife me,' he said grimly.

'No. I'm not saying any more – just that we want you over there.'

He arrived the next day, when the sun was high in a cloudless blue sky. Liza was waiting for him at the picket fence.

She was calm and pale-cheeked. She wore a simple dress with a floral pattern. Her hair gleamed like a raven's wing and was coiled neatly. She stood erectly and met his gaze with no trace of bitterness in her eyes.

'I want to say I'm sorry,' she said.

He took his hat off, confused and lost for words. 'Sarah has been making enquiries – she talked to the sheriff and it seems my father did meet with an accidental death. I'm a fool … and I'm sorry.'

'You don't have to talk like that; I understand.' He touched her arm. 'We've got a lot to say to each other, I reckon – and one thing we don't need to do is eat humble pie.'

'I'm bad-tempered.'

'So am I.'

'I'll never really be a lady.'

'You're one right now,' he told her. 'The best type. A lady with spirit…'

'All we'll ever do is fight…'

'Come on over to my ranch and make supper, then we'll see what we've got to fight about.'

'I'll never change. I'm a Backus, Matt Shayne.'

'That could be altered,' he said, then they began to laugh.

It was going to be a summer of change for both of them.

THE END

The publishers hope that this book has given you enjoyable reading. Large Print Books are especially designed to be as easy to see and hold as possible. If you wish a complete list of our books please ask at your local library or write directly to:

Dales Large Print Books
Magna House, Long Preston,
Skipton, North Yorkshire.
BD23 4ND

This Large Print Book, for people
who cannot read normal print,
is published under the auspices of
THE ULVERSCROFT FOUNDATION